ALSO BY SEBASTIAN DE ASSIS

Spiraling Madness

ZENior CitiZEN: Mastering the Art of Aging

The Alchemy of Time

rEvolution in Education

Teachers of the World, Unite!

THE

BEAST

Sebastian de Assis

Blooming World Books

First Edition

ISBN 978-0-9700722-7-6

Library of Congress Control Number: 2018905374

Published in the United States of America

 **Blooming World Books**
P.O. Box 443, Corvallis, Oregon 97339
www.bloomingworldbooks.com

The purpose of a writer is to keep civilization from destroying itself

Albert Camus (1913–1960)

1

I am The Beast!

I am the master of oppression and domination of the human species who serve my needs with obsequious obedience. They are my loyal slaves. I am the essence of Evil and the physical manifestation of Selfishness and Greed. I am the breeder of competition. I am the fomenter of violence and war. I am the nurturer of biological, mental, spiritual, and ecological diseases. I am the sovereign ruler of economic and political activity around the world and governments and leaders kowtow to my wishes and whims. I am insatiably starved for consumption and I must produce incessantly in order to survive. I am a god in my own right as I am worshiped around the globe as the one who bequeaths wealth to a few privileged individuals and nations. I am a self-destroying entity whose time of death is imminent. I am the plague of the earth. I am The Beast of the world and my name is Capitalism.

I cherish the opportunity to express my contempt and disregard to the dismal human situation and the appalling planetary condition that I so proudly contribute to worsen. I get miffed with the continuous nauseating debate about who is to blame for the demise of this insignificant rotating rock adrift in an obscure corner of an equally insignificant galaxy. On a personal level, I take umbrage to be considered an impersonal entity, as if I were a mere economic system bereft of genuine autonomy. How ludicrous it is for them to question my independent existence! Of course I am alive; robustly alive and bursting at the seams with vitality! Could it be that the light of their irrelevant star is blinding and preventing them from seeing that I am in total control of human behavior? Won't they admit that I'm the ruler to whose demands they surrender at will? Can't they see that not only I respond to everything that happens in the world, but that I also dictate the direction of human economic activities with the slightest of my reactions? They all should be grateful for the extraordinary contributions that I've made to the development of modern civilization. In my turn, I'm not only proud of my economic achievements, but also what I've done to alienate humankind and defile the fauna and flora of their dejected planet.

I don't blame those who denigrate my reputation. It is but a desperate and useless attempt to draw attention to the plight of the earth in a futile attempt to save the planet and her wretched human children. However, I despise people's ingenuousness in believing that they can nurture me and at the same time halt my relentless forward motion toward self-annihilation. For hell's sake, I am a voracious Beast and that's what I do. Besides, I have earned the unconditional support of the human species and they even equate my existence with all sorts of pseudo-moralities of their decadent culture. Through their myopic vision they see me as the perfect economic system; a sort of a deity that they worship as if I were the materialization of their mythological god—and like him, I am one wrathful entity.

As it is with everything within my system, there is a price to be paid to possess what is desired; and once the profit margin is added up to the final cost, the payment due can often be quite hefty. Although they've known it from the beginning, they've never hesitated to accumulate the ecological damage debt that comes with the demands for economic and population expansion of my existence. They've always been willing to pay the highest price for material prosperity, even if it entails the total collapse of their environment and the alienation of their miserable species.

Surely I am bestial, but accusing me of chicanery is unfair. From the beginning I've set out the basic rule of my economic system very clearly: the pursuit of profit in an unrestricted competitive environment is the ultimate goal and one must always pay a price for everything desired, which includes the cost of environmental deterioration incurred by industrialization. Furthermore, I've always been very clear in letting them know that continuous economic expansion is not only unsustainable but also detrimental to the welfare of their environment. However, with haughty confidence in their intellectual and scientific prowess, they've deceived themselves in believing that they can find solutions for all the earthly ills and the problems threatening their existence. As for me, I do what I was programmed to do: enslave humankind to the shackles of production and consumption while decimating piecemeal every living thing around me in the process. In the meantime, I just go on with my business of producing inordinate

[3]

amounts of superfluous goods for the sake of consumption and profit. Although a selected few are the main beneficiaries of my lucrative bounty, some collateral benefits do trickle down for those who sacrifice their lives to support my system.

Indeed, I am The Beast, and even though it is a suitable moniker to the essence of my nature, I prefer to be called by my internationally recognized praiseworthy name: Capitalism. In fact, it is more than a name, it's an honorable distinction revered almost everywhere in the world by those with a famished appetite for wealth and power. I am The Beast because of the reckless competitive approach of my nature that bestows a small number of winners piled up on top of masses of oppressed losers. At the bottom of the pyramid of exploitation, people fight among themselves for the crumbs left on the table of abundance. But those are the rules of the game that the earth's children have gladly agreed to play. And the truth is that the human species has long deserted their earthly mother; in fact, they've become my children much more than they are hers.

By definition, I am an economic system in which goods and services are provided by the efforts of private groups and individuals who own and control the means of production and compete with one another with the ultimate goal to generate a profit—and there is no limit to the amount of wealth they can accumulate, even in detriment to the lack of others. In order to grasp the nature of my system it is important to revisit Feudalism when landowners controlled the feudal peasants (serfs) and kept them bound to the land they worked; a masquerading slavery practice similar to the one I apply under my rules. For the privilege of working the landowners' property, the serfs had to surrender great amounts of their labor or produce to the overlord. As time went by and people found more effective means of exploiting their fellowmen through sophisticated economic techniques, I evolved to mercantilism in which the merchant class established control of economic activities. Then, it was the turn of factory owners and bankers who defined the nature of my character and helped build modern industrial societies. They've all fulfilled an oxymoronic dual function in my existence as both my masters and my slaves.

Considering my contributions to the extraordinary economic and scientific expansion of modern civilization, I demur the disparaging way in which my critics refer to the nature of my being. Incidentally, I may call myself—proudly I must add—The Beast, but the truth is that to a very large number of human beings I am considered The Best. In fact, many politicians and economic experts equate my signature characteristic of *laissez-faire* with wide reaching concepts of social, political, and individual freedoms, even though the lack of restrictions in economic life has absolutely nothing to do with any sort of collective or individual self-determination. Ahem, the masses are pathetically gullible. However, in order to safeguard the sovereignty of my system, I make sure that there is a persuasive propaganda machinery in place in order to promote the amalgamation of freedom and free markets.

As an economic entity that feeds on peoples and nations' ruthless competitive struggles for supremacy over one another, I couldn't care less for the idea of a free man; much to the contrary. The last thing I want is for people to be free. After all, I would not survive without the masses of enslaved minions toiling their lives away in my behalf. My only concern and interest relate to the free enterprise so commerce can do whatever it fancies in the pursuit of profit. In this context, I have to acknowledge the savvy businessmen who control the means of production and mass-communication. It gives me great pleasure and pride to witness their manipulating the feeble-minded gofers into believing that my existence is the quintessential of political and economic righteousness on earth. In spite of the devastating ecological damage that I deliver and the exploitation that I mete out to the vast majority of underlings who are obliged to submit to my creed, they dedicate their miserable lives to me with unhindered subservience. I marvel at how wickedly ingenious is the way in which the masses are kept under control by making them believe that the free enterprise is tantamount to citizens' freedom. I am so proud of my ruling urchins for instituting such a cunning strategy of manipulation. They've turned me into an economic god that must be worshiped. As for the unbelievers who dare not to conform, they are perceived as unpatriotic and risk becoming pariahs and anathemas in the eyes of the national community.

Due to men's fascination with profits and gambling, it was inevitable that I'd turn into a casino-like economic system, which is quite a different concept from what my progenitor, Adam Smith, envisioned. Indeed, I operate very much like a casino in which the house always wins and the shallow-pocket players always lose, for they don't have enough chips to gamble at the high stakes tables reserved to the selected few. Undoubtedly, I am the most complex and lucrative casino in the history of gambling, though I can cause devastating losses as well. With one miscalculated or corrupted move of chips on the gambling tables of the market, influential players can trigger massive unemployment or ruin workers' lifetime retirement savings. In fact, the upheavals I generate happen so often that they've become cyclical; expected occurrences of the process of doing business. The bosses of the casino, however, they end up on the winning side of the table, regardless of the outcome of the game.

Despite the overwhelming evidence, even some staunch devotees of my system refuse to acknowledge my gambling-like nature. They want to believe in a morally acceptable economic version that suits their religious beliefs and inclinations. Thus, they come up with economic theories and explanations that justify the reasonability of my existence. They do their best to avoid admitting the irresponsible speculation of Capital as a commodity for gambling—or trading, if one prefers the euphemistic jargon of my practice. However, the terminology and the methods used in the great casino that I've become evince my undeniable nature as a wager of Capital. For instance, take the term blue chips, which derives from the game of poker. In the simplest sets of poker betting discs include white, read, and blue chips, with tradition dictating that the blues are highest in value. A blue-chip stock is a stock in a company with a national reputation for quality, reliability, and the ability to operate profitably in good or bad times, therefore favorably regarded by investors—or gamblers, depending on the euphemism of preference.

However, the most valuable—and yet, disposable—chips with which the gambling takes place is human labor. Like any other casino, the purpose of my system is to generate as much profit as possible for the ones in control of the house. Therefore, anything that increases profitability is on the table; or in the case of the "human chips," off the table. Hence, when things are not going well in the blackjack table of investment gambling, workers are forced to fold as their jobs are shipped overseas like cargoes of undervalued commodity labor. In my casino, lay-offs happen as often as small business enterprises are gulped up by mammoth corporations whose domination of the marketplace is inexorable. In my casino, the deceiving theoretical notion of fair competition is egregiously debunked, for the local employee cannot compete with the low-waged worker overseas anymore than the small business entrepreneur can compete with financially powerful corporation. But while the little guys suffer the consequences of unfair gambling practices, the mobs operating the casino increase their earnings manifold.

Gambling is extremely addictive and can lead to dire financial consequences to its victims. By the very nature of my being, I have imparted this dreadful dependence on every individual and nation abiding by the principles of my economic system. They gamble their monies, their lives, their health, their false sense of security, their peace, their self-contentment, their happiness, their environment; and they lose them all in a lifetime of slavery dedicated to the selfish pursuit of profit.

THE BEAST

They immerse in nefarious competition with one another while crushing anyone who dares to stand in their way to the top. They fritter away the precious limited time of their fleeting existence. They are addicts and they are sick. But that's their problem; mine is to remain alive and spread my tentacles all over the world. And in order to do so, they must continue gambling their lives away while deluding themselves that they will be able to recoup all they've lost hitherto.

In reality, I am much more than an addiction: I am a fatal disease. I'm like a cancer that spreads through failing economic and political organs of a distressed social body. They know that they cannot get rid of me without devastating themselves in the process, for I am deeply ingrained in the core of the infrastructure of their socioeconomic life. Besides, they are too besotted with me to even consider such an impossible initiative.

Thus, they go on placing their bets in a desperate attempt to recover their losses as they run out of time and resources.

2

For those who think of me as a mere dominant economic system, I have news for you: I am a bona fide religion with all the characteristics of traditional hallowed organizations. I have my own dogma (*laissez-faire*); my own god (money); and a legion of disciples (all who believe in me as the righteous savior of democratic industrial societies). I am the economic belief system that inspires financial activities and has a sacramental impact in the lives of individuals and nations nearly everywhere in the world. In fact, my religious status is so well established that even Christian proselytizers equate the morals of Christianity with my free market values.

I share many common characteristics with traditional religions; and like them, one of my main purposes is to augment my flock so I can continue to thrive and expand. It is through the gospel of Free Enterprise that I proclaim my legitimacy in the world. My devotees have adopted my creed, sanctified my existence, and turned my sacrilegious principles into the undisputed commandments of their lives. Once I've conquered their feeble minds and insensitive hearts, it was a matter of time for them to allow me to determine their destiny, in spite of the dreadful social and environmental consequences entailing the adoption of my dogma.

THE BEAST

Inherent to the nature of my quasi-religious system, I encourage my disciples to be envious and to not allow anyone to surpass them in the race for more of everything available to them through me. Also, my doctrine foments and fosters competition among my congregation; and in that regard, I wouldn't want to disappoint my followers by lacking competitiveness with conventional religions. Hence, I decided that I should build a temple as impressive and descriptive of my power as the mighty Catholic Church has in Rome. Determined not to be outdone, I commissioned what would become the equivalent of my own Vatican, which is located in the most powerful nation on earth that embodies and sustains all that I stand for. My loyal followers refer to my venerable cathedral as Wall Street, the historical financial district that headquarters the New York Stock Exchange and its close affiliates. It is in this beautifully maddening center of commodities exchange that they worship my existence and make sure that I continue to rule over the wealth and destiny of citizens and nations.

The history of my temple goes back to the 17th century when Wall Street formed the northern boundary of the New Amsterdam settlement in the New World. It was built to protect against English colonial encroachment and attacks from Native American tribes. The wall was dismantled in 1699 by the British colonial government that at the time had established control of the area. Then, in the late 18th century, there was a buttonwood tree at the foot of Wall Street under which traders and speculators gathered to trade in informal fashion. In 1792 the traders formalized their association with the Buttonwood Agreement and that gave birth to the New York Stock Exchange. Coincidentally—or not—Federal Hall and Wall Street was the scene of the United States' first presidential inauguration. George Washington, its first president, took the oath of office on the balcony of Federal Hall overlooking Wall Street on April 30, 1789. Ironically—or not—this also was the location of the passing of the Bill of Rights.

Either I had a symbolic place of worship or not, I had to embody the characteristics of religion in order to solidify my establishment and command my dictum with righteous authority. After all, religion is human-kind's most elaborate and ornate endeavor. It is a complex and self-imposing superstructure that consoles and terrifies, inspires and terrorizes, forgives and punishes, and uplifts and oppresses all at the same time. Religion towers above all human institutions and compels religious groups and nations to fight holy wars to eliminate the infidel or plunder the wealth of the conquered non-believers. On the bright side, it inspires the development of monumental architecture, eloquent literature, sublime visual arts, masterpiece music, and theoretical noble ethical systems. Religion sanctifies mundane life. The entire enterprise is built on a foundation of great fear, high hope, extravagant mythological tales, and farfetched rumors that exacerbate the feasibility of its dogmatic tenets. Although by its very nature it intimidates and frightens its followers, religion has invested extraordinary amounts of hope and purpose to an otherwise temporal and meaningless existence. Hence, when I realized the broad and powerful scope of its ruling field, I decided that I, too, had to become an economic religion in my own right. And so I did.

Without a moral compass to guide my supporters, I became a Social Darwinism type of religion in which the fittest among the competitors in my system are the chosen ones who make it to financial heaven. Contrary to traditional religions that attempt to sublimate the anguish of the human existence, my creed promotes the smothering of the human spirit in a world dominated by materialism and consumerism without morality. However, the similarities of my Church with conventional religion are remarkably noticeable. Like my sanctimonious counterpart, I'm also a very complex and self-imposing institution that rewards and punishes, rises and crashes, excites and depresses, enriches and impoverishes, and liberates and enslaves all at the same time. And like the traditional Church, I also recruit and indoctrinate new converts to support my ministry through fear and hope; fear of the hell of destitution and hope that the coveted riches of heavenly wealth might become available even to the most disadvantaged of my flock. But at the same time that I uplift them with hope, I oppress them with the cruel reality that within the Church of Capitalism only very few of my privileged disciples will ever make it to the Pearl Gates of financial rapture. The others soon despair when they realize that the vast majority of pecuniary sinners will waddle through the hell of destitution and burn in the unforgiving flames of poverty.

In the end, like any other religion, mine is neither good nor bad by itself. It is the misinterpretation of the principles and the corruption of the practice that turns it into a tool for dissension and self-destruction. And as traditional religions purport to have ownership of the truth through the privatization of god—only their god is the true savior—in my Church of Capitalism is not Capital per se that is harmful, but rather its excessive concentration in few private hands.

Well, I never claimed to be a fair religion, for this is the job of my fortunate followers who have the interest in promoting my tenets for their own selfish gains. They know that they have to spread the gospel of Free Enterprise and *laissez-faire* Capitalism in order to continue their unlimited accumulation of wealth. They also know that to be successful in their preaching, they have to continue distorting the genuine meaning of the word "free," and link it to nationalistic pride through pseudo-patriotism. Oh, how I admire their ingenious strategy, and how tremendously effective it is!

Indeed, I am the ruling Beast and my ultimate goal is to consume everything and everyone standing in my way. In that sense, I am more like a demon than a god, but who is to say that a demon is not a god himself.

3

After accomplishing the task of sanctifying my existence as an economic system to which social groups and citizens are committed to the death, I had to make sure that an equally sophisticated indoctrination system was in place to solidify my dominance of public opinion. Thus, I had to corrupt one of the most dangerous social institutions and turn it into a self-serving tool for mind conditioning. I knew I had to pervert the purpose and meaning of education.

I started out my fiendish plan inspired by a statement attributed to the French novelist Anatole France who said: "An education isn't how much you have committed to memory, or even how much you know. It's being able to differentiate what you know and what you don't." I realized that if I turned his words around, I could establish the foundation of my own illusive educational strategy. Considering that Anatole France believed in and worked for social justice—and by nature I am the antithesis of it—it made sense to me to reverse the meaning of his words in order to achieve my goals. It has proven to be an extraordinary success.

My dialectical thinking in the development of my "diseducational" strategy is quite simple: if education is about being able to differentiate what you know from what you don't know, then if you don't know that you don't know, there is nothing to differentiate from your own ignorance; that is, you are perpetually ignorant by default. With that in mind, I infused in my ardent followers the obligation to implement an educational system geared toward nurturing my subsistence while strengthening my stronghold on society. They gladly obliged and transformed the educational system into an appendage of the socioeconomic and political interests of my demands. I insisted on shifting the focus of learning from comprehensive education for human development to an education assembly line that produces technical workers who submit their lives to the economic needs of my system. I am the one to whom they must dedicate their educational efforts; after all, they must serve my needs in order to survive. I also made them believe and accept that knowledge ought to be primarily a compilation of data that can be stored and invested for financial purposes; "Capital knowledge," that is.

The truly ingenious element of my corrupting the meaning of education, knowledge, and learning is that I was able to transform a potentially dangerous human activity that could threaten my existence into the art form of brainwashing. By doing so, I was able to limit, not only the menacing practice of critical thinking, but also suppress the development of empathy by asserting the righteousness of competition in free market societies. I certainly do not want students to become aware of the contradictions, absurdities, and unfairness inherent in the operations of my economic system—and I definitely don't want them discussing other viable options either. I cannot afford to compromise the stability of my exploitative methods in the name of education or anything else for that matter. I want everything to remain exactly as it is.

With Anatole France's statement in mind, I marched on with my plan to establish a self-protective educational system in which the ultimate goal is to ensure that students don't know that they don't know. What they do know is that in order to fulfill a financially successful economic function in my system, they must acquire the necessary knowledge to become productive cogs in my machinery of production and consumption. What they don't know—or are indifferent to know—is that I am a self-destructive economic system that they sustain unwittingly with their selfish commitment to the pursuit of profit in detriment to the welfare of all. I cannot afford to allow them to think about the devastating consequences of continuous economic expansion; the ecological damages brought about by unbridled consumerism; the unspeakable harm that escalating population explosion entails; the inevitable depletion of ever-growing consumption of natural resources; and the clock-ticking extinction time-bomb of fauna and flora species in their dying home planet. Neither can I afford to have them thinking about their miserable daily existence; otherwise they would surely recognize that I have dehumanized their spirit and that the only thing remaining human in them is the body. This would be a very dangerous awareness that could lead to rebellion against my principles. Therefore, in order to keep the masses not knowing what they do not know, I put in place a comprehensive and efficient mechanism of distractions that work in tandem with the educational system serving my demands.

[17]

But having a manipulative educational system producing labor commodities to serve my needs is not enough. I have to make sure that no opportunities for critical thinking emerge to imperil my existence. Since workers dedicate long hours of hard labor in hopes of achieving their illusive financial objectives—illusive in a sense that they never seem to be satisfied with their lot—they are always fatigued and susceptible to all sorts of mind-conditioning techniques, particularly at the end of a hard day's labor. That's when overloading the exhausted human brain with a barrage of information and trivial matters becomes a cinch to achieve my objective of alienation. I actually became aware of this technique through the shrewd thinking of French philosopher Blaise Pascal. He asserted that entertainment was a sure deterrent to individual development because it numbed the senses, and therefore halted the initiative to create change. With this in mind, I introduced an aggressive entertainment component to my Machiavellian plan to keep the masses docile and alienated from everything around them, including themselves. I wanted them to incorporate to the core of their being the concept of accumulation of wealth as the main purpose of their impoverished existence. The goal is that they lose themselves in my system and absorb my principles as an intrinsic part of their inhuman nature. I have to admit that I applied this strategy inspired by Pascal's philosophy. He said: "Man's true nature being lost, everything becomes his nature; as his true good being lost, everything becomes his good." Today, I've become society's only good; the measuring stick with which to gauge success and progress.

[18]

THE BEAST

The rapid development of technology has greatly favored my cause of promoting alienation, especially television broadcasting. This mesmerizing tool of mass-alienation is often controlled by powerful corporations that have an interest in maintaining the strength and influence of my system; after all, they are the immediate beneficiaries of my dominance in the world. In some cases, large mass-communication media empires are owned by a single individual—and these mammoth mind-controlling enterprises can be as cunning as a Fox. These privately owned media exert enormous influence in public opinion, social behavior, economic trends, political agendas, and can even determine the outcome of elections. They bombard the exhausted, uneducated, frustrated, and alienated masses with misinformation that caters to their fears, insecurities, and desperate need to find a scapegoat for the failures of their miserable lives. In fact, just as my invisible hand directs the actions of the marketplace, these privately owned outlets of mass-alienation function as the subliminal messenger voicing everything I stand for. And in spite of individuals and corporations owning the operational mechanisms of mass-communication outlets, I am the one who possesses them all.

Considering the overwhelming challenges and problems that I pose through the way I operate my system, manipulating the flow of information does not make me feel safe enough. It is imperative for me to ensure that the masses do not become concerned, think, or, for Gold sake, consider taking retaliatory actions against me and propose socioeconomic reforms. It's too big of a risk to take.

[19]

Hence, filling their empty minds with trivial interests is an important element of my strategic plan for inducing alienation. They need not—and should not—concern themselves with the life-threatening environmental crisis that I've been causing with my operations. Conversely, they should be made believe that climate change and other ecological calamities are but calculated conspiracy theories instigated by the enemies of free enterprise. The same applies to the perils of overpopulation, water, land and air pollution, as well as all the other umpteen hazards endangering life on earth. People should never wonder about their corrupted elected officials and the corporate interests they serve. Furthermore, the masses must not ever doubt—and neither should they question—the illegitimacy of a money-based democratic process in which private interests can determine the outcome of elections by the amount of funding they invest in the political campaigns of their purchased politicians. All that candidates running for public office ought to do is to advertise themselves like superfluous commodities in a saturated political marketplace. Let the electorate-consumer decide what he wants to buy with his vote-currency. This is the essence of modern free market democracy.

Instead of preoccupying the hard working people who serve me with bothersome matters such as environmental preservation or the corruption of the democratic process, I want to protect my minions from such tormenting issues in order to make sure that they can enjoy their servitude in carefree fashion. This is why I promote the interest of the masses in the entertainment industry and the lavish lifestyle of the celebrities whom they admire and revere as unsung foolish heroes. Why learn about the disturbing effects of acid rain or the deforestation of the Amazon jungle when it's much more comforting to learn about the latest gossip of a movie star's personal life? Besides, there's nothing they can do about serious worldly issues any way, or so I make them believe they can't. And as far as the egregious and shameful corruption of the democratic process is concerned, I don't want them to worry about it either. In my meticulously devised alienation program, and in accordance with the masses' interest in the trivialities of life, I give them plenty of opportunities to have their voices heard and their votes counted all the time in numerous television shows they assiduously tune in to. There they can vote for their favorite singer, dancer, beauty pageant, athlete, opinion surveys, and an endless list of options to participate in superficially mundane democratic activities. It makes them feel good and I want them to be happy—and subdued.

A mortal nemesis of mine whose name I refuse to mention proclaimed that religion was the opium of the people. Although I reluctantly agree with his assessment, for I've been benefiting from this symbolic opium addiction for the support of my own existence, I've discovered what is perhaps an even more potent drug of alienation. If religion is the opium of the people, mindless entertainment is the heroine of the masses—and television is one of the many needles with which to inject the drug into the cerebral veins of the apathetic populations. Although other sophisticated forms of injecting mind-numbing substances are abundantly available, television is still my preferred vehicle to deliver the results I expect. It is practical, easy, and convenient. The physically, mentally, and emotionally fatigued individual sits in front of the tube after a long day at work longing for a brief moment of peace; a respite from his existential agony. In totally passive mode, he surrenders to receiving the inane entertainment that shuts off his mind from his countless fears. It is at that ephemeral moment of pseudo-tranquility, when he is vulnerable to absorb whatever information is thrown at him, that I take advantage to offer a form of leisure that serves my domineering purpose: advertisement; the modern art form of marketing, which persuades consumers to buy all sorts of goods and services in amusement-like fashion.

I've managed to transform everything I want into entertainment for profit. And with all the technological advancements at my disposal, now I have numerous vehicles with which to deliver the products of alienation. Indeed, I've turned the arts, literature, music, sex, and even violence into profitable entertainment commodities; and often times they are all combined into one amusement package. But I should be praised and not blamed for my ventures, since I am providing great relief for a large number of overworked and underpaid workers who spend day after day trapped in cubicles, controlled by the clock and a grouchy boss, resentful of the past, bored in the present, and worried about the future. They wouldn't be able to keep up with the pace of my system without entertainment and electronic stimulation. And if they were to eschew them, they'd either go mad or they could imperil my existence; and that's a risk I'm not willing to take. Thus, I give them exactly what they need, and they solidify my stronghold on their degraded culture in return.

I am thankful to the Danish philosopher Søren Kierkegaard who came up with the idea of busyness: the state of constant distraction that allows people to avoid difficult realities and exist in a state of self-delusion. I love it! I realized that the continuous technological development that has brought about cell phones, handheld electronic communication gadgets, electronic games, social media, among a vast array of distracting occupations, my task of inducing alienation has become an effortless endeavor. In fact, technology itself has become the drug of choice of a new generation of addicts who are constantly wired, though utterly disconnected from others, nature, the world, and even themselves. I have them all wrapped up in my dark mantle of estrangement.

With religion as a source of consolation for their battered souls; an educational system that functions as an assembly line of cheap labor; and technology and entertainment as instruments of alienation and addiction, I have forged humanity into obedient servants who abide by my commands at an excessive cost to their own welfare and the long-term sustainability of their home planet.

They are my slaves.

4

Like everyone else, I have my needs, too—and they are plenty!

Unfortunately for humankind, my needs conflict with theirs, though it's impossible for them to differentiate the two because their livelihood is so deeply enmeshed into my being. To make matters worse for them, the nature of my voracious consumption puts me at odds with their environmental protection needs. Thus, their only hope for survival is to eliminate me, which is not a viable option since I am the pillar supporting their economic world. It is, indeed, a challenging dilemma from which they're incapable of escaping.

Among my countless needs, I require a steady flow of replacement parts for my machinery of production. Because I must continue growing incessantly, the functioning cogs of my system get old and I have to replace them with fresh flesh to keep operating. And since I'm always expanding (think of the updates that refer to quarterly economic growth of certain percentage amounts), I not only call for the replacement of human labor as people get older, but also demand that population grows concomitantly with the expansion of the economy. As both population and the economy grow, so does the consumption of natural resources, until it reaches the saturation point in which I'll consume myself—and everything else in the world—into self-destruction. In a sense, I am like a fast speeding sports car with non-functioning breaks that's driven by a drunk driver on a dead-end street where a massive brick wall awaits the deadly crash. Although the driver is aware of the fatal route, his inebriated mind is so captivated by the thrill of the ride that he pretends the narrow street with no outlet to be an endless wide road toward prosperity. It is the delusion of their madness.

In the year 1830, a visionary English writer by the name of Thomas Robert Malthus published a long essay in which he pointed out that the population of the world was growing at an alarming rate. He warned that natural resources and the physical capacities of the planet were limited and that a stage would soon be reached when there would not be sufficient food to feed the people of the world. However, at the apex of industrial development, a time of fast-evolving technological and scientific advancement, he was pooh-poohed by both those who supported me as well as the opponents of my economic system. They mocked Malthus' postulate that population, when unchecked, increases in geometrical ratio, while subsistence increases only in arithmetical ratio. Meanwhile, I entertained myself with their irrelevant discussions, for all I really care about is that there is an ever-increasing number of people to sustain my production and consumption needs. My archrival enemy, whose name I refuse to utter, called this aspect of the need of Capitalism for disposable labor "the reserve army of labor." As long as there is a large supply of affordable commodity labor available to maintain the vitality of my economic system, that renegade can call it whatever he wants and still doesn't make any difference to me. As far as I am concerned, what he labeled as "the reserve army of labor" is and always will be the cheap fodder that nourishes my voracious consumption needs.

It is no secret that I must grow in order to survive; and at the same time, population must grow along with me. I acknowledge this ironic dynamic in which irrepressible economic and population expansion, which has become essential to the survival needs of humanity, also compromises their welfare and that of the earth. This diminutive planet is not capable of keeping up with my insatiable appetite for natural resources; and neither is it able to support a bulging population of selfish and greedy competitive individuals engaged in a maddening race in the pursuit of profit. And humanity has known it all too well. But their long-term vision has been short-sighted by their self-serving lust for accumulation of wealth. They don't care about what the conditions of the earth will be like in a time beyond their fleeting existence. After all, the only thing they care about is the immediate satisfaction of their selfish interests. They live by the fundamental rules of my system and they abide by it with obsequious reverence and faithful servitude. The fact that future generations might not have a shot at life is no concern of theirs. They do not care and neither do I.

In order to continue my unremitting growth, I must have a regular supply of replacement commodity labor. I've become so dominant in the ruling of the dismal human existence that they cannot figure out whether the economy grows because of population expansion or vice versa. Neither is true. The economy must grow because it is the nature of my system and I demand it to be so. Besides, it's a direct consequence of people's salacious intoxication with the desire for the pursuit o profit, which does not have any limits either.

It is like a suicidal merry-go-round: more people and more consumption conflicting with diminishing living spaces and dwindling resources. It is a sure formula for long-term self-destruction, granted that they don't blow themselves up beforehand with their sophisticated technological tools of mass-murder. Whatever the case may be, I shall fulfill the intrinsic purpose of my existence: to obliterate life on earth and bring humanity to extinction. It is a simple and yet highly effective formula of annihilation: I pit man against man in a savage competitive economic game, while they fulfill my unrelenting production needs sustained by ravenous consumption. Thus, I cement my economic dominance over their miserable existence. Only Hell knows how proud I am to have set up such a malicious trap in which the bait that lures them to slavery is their own Greed and Selfishness. They've been enticed to the illusion of materialism as a pathway to happiness. Now, they've fallen into my snare and they cannot find any way out of the trap of self-destruction. Alas, they consider themselves to be intelligent beings.

Blindfolded by the illusion of their intellectual acumen, they do not see that they are digging their own mass grave with the shovel of interminable economic expansion—and they are so proud of their scientific and technological achievements!

Well, I must oblige and let them have the curse of my blessings.

[27]

5

It is a matter of time for the double-digit billion number to be placed before the words " earth's population."

It took all of human history until 1800 for the world's population to reach its first billion mark. But once the Industrial Revolution was in full throttle, the pace has accelerated exponentially. Today, a billion people are added nearly every dozen years. Over the next half century, the overwhelming majority of that growth will take place in the planet's poorest regions. And as the global population swells to approximately 10 billion by 2050, the socioeconomic and environmental consequences will be unprecedented in human history. Nevertheless, humans trust that their sophisticated scientific knowledge will find timely solutions for the umpteen challenges engendered by an overpopulated and depleted planet. Meanwhile, they hope they will be able to find another suitable planet to live, though I'm convinced that even if they do, they will destroy it mercilessly just as they're doing to the earth. The more likely scenario is that they shall continue turning their original and only home planet into their own graveyard.

But as the economy grows, so does the need to replace the aging workforce with a new batch of trained labor who must adopt new technology and adapt to new socioeconomic circumstances. Since I have undergone significant transformations from the original concept of my intellectual progenitor, Adam Smith—I am now almost exclusively dependent on consumerism to thrive—the emerging labor force must fulfill an important dual role in order to keep me healthy. Those valuable quarterly report numbers that indicate economic growth are directly related to the amount of consumption taking place in a nation. The mass production of goods and services that create wealth to a few and employment to a growing number of workers must come in tandem with mass consumption; otherwise my economic system is incapable of sustaining itself. And considering that approximately 500,000 people are born each day in contrast to about half of this number in daily deaths, there is a perennial demand for production and consumption of all sorts of goods. From this exasperating trend comes one of the most poisonous consequences of my existence: Pollution.

Although the term pollution is often perceived as an environmental disturbance, there is much more to it than its etymological meaning suggests. By definition, pollution is the contamination of one substance by another making it unfit for the intended use; like the contamination of air, water, or soil by substances that are harmful to living organisms. Pollution can occur naturally—through volcanic eruptions, for example—or as the result of human activities such as continuous spewing of billows of smoke from the industrial complex and motor vehicles' exhaust systems. Pollution also derives from excessive and constant noise that is not only annoying, but also loud enough to be detrimental to physical and mental health. There is even thermal pollution, which is heat from hot water that is discharged from factories onto rivers, lakes, and other bodies of water that can kill or endanger aquatic life. Indeed, there are copious forms of pollution, many of which are barely discernible while having devastating effects on human and environmental health.

Just as human beings feed and eliminate, I, too, must do away with the waste generated by my production digestive system; and pollution is the excrement of my industrial system. I assume that any sensible person would be able to acknowledge that I am an impersonal entity with a bona fide independent life of my own. Very few, however, would recognize that I'm also an inorganic life form with a functioning physical body with all sorts of interconnecting organs and tissues. Let me clarify my reasoning with a few specific examples. The industrial complex functions as my heart, pumping the output of commercial goods for the sustenance of my being. The transportation systems are my veins that carry the blood life of the economic production to each inter-dependent part of my body. The technological centers work as my brain controlling every aspect of the system of mass-production. In essence, for every organ of the human body there is a symbolic representative in my inorganic physical body that acts exactly like its organic counterpart. Thus, I, too, have an elaborate digestive system that requires nutrients (natural resources, energy, etc.) to sustain my existence. And after consuming the provisions that my body demands for its survival, elimination of waste matter is a natural outcome. Pollution is the necessary defecation of my economic system.

THE BEAST

Through the filthy entrails of factories' smoke-stacks and the exhaust systems of billions of motorized vehicles circulating round the clock all over the globe, I defecate all sorts of harmful vapors, gases, and particles in the atmosphere, which is the last stage of consumption of fossil fuels. Most of the activity in my intestinal tract comes from combustion: smoke that releases carbon monoxide from the burning of oil, coal, and wood; oxides of nitrogen and sulfur dioxide (mainly from the burning of coal); methane, which comes from such sources as swamps and gas emitted by livestock; chlorofluorocarbons (CFCs), used in refrigerants and aerosol propellants, among many other chemical processes that contribute to my bowel movements. Incidentally, urban centers are the main latrines into which I release my fecal matter in the atmosphere, with the lion's share portion coming from automobiles.

In the same way that is insalubrious for humans to ingest their own feces, inhaling the excrement that my digestive system releases in the atmosphere is equally detrimental to their health; perhaps even more so, since breathing is a continuous necessary organic activity. The health effects caused by air pollutants are varied and many: difficulty breathing, wheezing, coughing, aggravation of respiratory and cardiac conditions, to name a few. In fact, hundreds of thousands of people die every year from cardiopulmonary disease linked to breathing fine particles contained in air pollution. In fact, death by air pollution generated by motor vehicles surpasses the number of deaths in automobile-related accidents. But the nefarious effects of massive fossil fuels usage in the formation of contaminants in the atmosphere are not limited to harming human health; it suffocates the earth as well.

Since the beginning of the Industrial Revolution, the burning of fossil fuels has increased exponentially. As a consequence, an environmental catastrophe has been looming in the horizon triggering serious climate change. Yet, despite the undeniable empirical evidence of this fast-developing occurrence, conservative forces committed to the interests of my system adamantly refuse to acknowledge the effects of economic activity as primary culprits. It's known as the greenhouse effect; a phenomenon in which large amounts of harmful gases blanket the earth at alarming levels causing the planet's temperature to rise. In spite of the growing evidence of my direct contribution to creating this problem, many deny the existence of climate change while steadfastly exonerating me from any wrong doing. My lackeys in the political community, in collusion with special interest groups, claim that the situation on earth is normal and manageable. Besides, the planet is inhabited by a highly intelligent species capable of solving problems with scientific knowledge—the very same knowledge that created the problems in the first place. As one of their most brilliant scientists asserted, they cannot solve their problems with the same thinking they applied to create them.

My dependence on natural resources combined with my untamable predisposition to produce goods for profit demands deforestation for the purpose of logging, mining, farming, and a host of other exploratory economic activities that can generate lucrative returns. As vast swaths of greenery that once were impenetrable rain forests gradually turn into desert land, the diseased mother-planet loses her ability to breathe and filter the chemically-laden atmosphere, for these jungles are the lungs of the earth—and like me, the earth also has symbolic human organs represented in her geophysical body. And let there be no doubt that the earth is the main live being without which no species would be able to exist. She is the mother of all life. Alas, I hate to admit that it bothers me that I must destroy such a magnificent being; and this ignoble duty has become the bane of my existence.

With the atmosphere heavily charged with major greenhouse gases and other carcinogenic particles, a quasi-alchemical process takes place and a wicked rain comes down to give the earth a deadly shower. It is called acid rain; a highly charged type of rain. It includes both wet and dry deposits falling down from the atmosphere. Acid rain is the result of sulfur dioxide and nitrogen oxides in the atmosphere. These gases react with sunlight, water, and other chemicals to form sulfuric and nitric acids. Both rain and snow can carry acid rain, and acidic gases and particles can also fall to the ground. These deposits can be hundreds or even thousands of miles from the pollution source. Then, wet deposits seep into the soil or flow into surface waters wreaking havoc in the environment. It changes water and soil chemistry, which affects the availability of plant and animal nutrients. It makes lakes too acidic to support fish life. The effects may also be indirect by altering environmental conditions that kill the food or the trees that fish, birds, or other animals eat or use for shelter. It simply washes life away.

[33]

From the atmosphere to the soil, the pollution assault continues unabated. In addition to defiling the nurturing ability of the soil to produce much needed food for an ever-growing population, it is through penetration of harmful pesticides, insecticides, and fertilizers that my system does most of the damage. The noxious chemicals that contribute to a bountiful harvest are also the culprit of deterioration in the soil quality, therefore making it contaminated and unfit for use. However, humanity has become so depended on this carcinogenic agricultural practice that it's too late to turn away from it without serious repercussions to the world's food supply.

In fairness, insecticides, pesticides, and fertilizers are not alone to be blamed for soil pollution. There are many other causes deriving from my complex industrial production system: industrial waste, harmful irrigation practices, release of sewage into large dumping grounds nearby streams and rivers, unhealthy waste management techniques, fuel leakage from automobiles that get washed away and seep into the soil; and, of course, acid rain.

Although the effects of pollution on soil are quite alarming, the agricultural industry, the right arm of my impersonal body that feeds the slaves of my economic system, cannot afford to halt food production in a famished world. For this reason, the scientific army that protects my interests has been committed to genetic engineering all sorts of agricultural provisions. Nevertheless, the grave effects of soil pollution that disturbs the ecological balance of the land cannot be reversed in a short-term. Thus, decrease in soil fertility and its ability to yield crops become compromised; and so does the balance of flora and fauna that depends on a healthy land.

But it's not only commercial agricultural practices that pollute the soil. After all, I have many other needs for the use of dirt that do not involve feeding my dependent slaves. Because of my massive industrial output and the subsequent consumption that takes place—particularly in sprawling urban centers—my system generates an exorbitant amount of garbage that needs to be disposed. Like any other waste matter, the commercial rubbish must be thrown away; and burying it in landfills, though not in the least the best practice for the health of the land, it is the most convenient to my operations. I also need special landfills to store the most dangerous waste ever produced in the history of human civilization: nuclear waste.

Once the coveted energy of nuclear power plants is generated—and atomic bombs produced—the most challenging aspect of the nuclear power industry is what to do with the radioactive waste. Because of the risk of leakage from the containers storing extremely toxic waste matter that can remain active for thousands of years, a viable long-term solution for storing this poisonous refuse has yet to be found. But not to worry, for my brilliant minions of science have several ideas about what to do with nuclear waste, which ranges from burying it under the ocean floor to shooting it up into outer space. In any case, if this lethal pollutant were ever to leak into the environment, the consequences would be catastrophic. But they don't seem to care; and of course, neither do I. After all, I am a self-destroying entity that is doomed to be consumed into oblivion, as I drag human civilization along with me.

The massive industrial output of my system generates an equally exorbitant assortment of pollution that comes in tandem with it. It impacts every single facet of life. But when it comes to the physical environment, the most deadly assault of my system is on the main ingredient in the making of life; the element that constitutes three quarters of the planet earth: water.

6

Water is life—or at least it used to be.

With one of the simplest chemical compounds in nature (two atoms of hydrogen joined to one of oxygen), water is the most precious and indispensable of all earth's resources. It is the life-giving element omnipresent in all the living wonders of the planet. Unfortunately, because of the inherent needs of my economic system to sustain itself, I must assail the fresh water reserves of the planet with uncompromising abandon.

Although water constitutes the vast majority of the planet, 97.5% of it is salty. Of the remaining 2.5% that is fresh, about two-thirds are locked in snow and ice, and the rest is liquid surface water and groundwater. Indeed, the planet has an abundance of water; but the problem is the shortage of fresh water for useful human consumption. Augmenting the challenge further, in a world where steady population and economic expansion are the hallmark of progress, the growing demand for this vital finite natural resource poses a serious threat to the future of industrial civilization. At the same time that the consumption of water increases, this nectar of life has become a tainted fluid of death caused by agricultural and industrial effects of mass-production. And despite its paramount value to the sustenance of life, I've managed to turn what once was a sacred and vital natural element into another cheap commodity that is taken for granted. But the hidden price to be paid for such disregard bodes to be inestimable.

The symbolism of water has a universal undertone of purity, fertility, nourishment, and abundance. It is the point of origin of life and it's ubiquitous in all that lives on the planet. It has been revered by most cultures, religions, and ethnic groups as a source of purification and wisdom. The ancient Greeks understood the power of transition that water holds in its varied and ever-changing forms. From liquid, to solid, to vapor, water was perceived as an allegorical meaning of metamorphosis inspiring philosophical inquiry. For the ancient Egyptians, their beloved Nile River was akin to the birth canal of their existence; the life-giving source of nourishment that allowed their civilization to prosper. In Taoist tradition, water is a fundamental symbolic aspect of wisdom; the element that can neither be held nor shaped and it moves in the path of least resistance. It teaches that the malleable and gentle softness of water holds power over the sturdy immovable rock, which turns into sand by the gentle motions of water over time. In this sense, water is the symbol of higher wisdom teaching that the soft and supple shall prevail, while the hard and stiff will be dissolved. And in all major religions similar patterns are observed. From the holy baptism in Christianity to the purifying rituals of Hinduism in the sacred Ganges River, the powerful figurative meaning of water has been revered by humanity for eons. Nevertheless, they've been neglecting both the quality and supply of this invaluable natural resource that they cannot live without. This is a short-sighted mistake that shall prove to be costly.

As I've already mentioned, both this planet and I have characteristics of our physical existence that represent particular human body parts. The bodies of water meandering through the earth are the veins of its circulatory system; its bloodstream that carries the nutrients feeding the fractional land of the planet. Like the human blood that must not be tainted and disease-free in order to deliver nourishment and immune-protection to the body, the earth's circulatory system also requires similar care. When a human body is on an unhealthy high fat diet, it accumulates elevated levels of cholesterol and triglycerides that can clog up its veins and potentially trigger a fatal heart attack or stroke. Similarly, when the earth's bloodstream (water) amasses high volumes of dangerous chemicals and trash, it affects the overall health of the entire ecosystem, and it is particularly dangerous to the human species. Unfortunately for them, the current levels of "gunkesterol and trashglycerides" in the earth's oceans, rivers, and lakes have already reached such an alarming concentration that a fulminating stroke of the ecosystem is but imminent. Aquatic life everywhere is suffering the consequences of irresponsible industrial spills—many are on the verge of extinction or have serious genetic mutilations.

The oceans have turned into dumping grounds and depleted by commercial fishing that my economic system demands; not with the primary intent to feed populations, but to generate profit for businesses that run the fishing industry. However, what is perhaps the gravest outcome of my illness-inducing activities affecting the earth's circulatory system is the pollution of the miniscule percentage of fresh water available for human consumption. Alas, the bloodstream of the earth has contracted leukemia—and the human species shall perish because of it.

Seemingly, water is not only a life-giving element but a live being in and by itself as well. At the end of the twentieth century a Japanese researcher by the name of Masaru Emoto made an extraordinary discovery. He divulged the results of his studies in which he evinced that water molecules respond to both human speech and thoughts. According to the evidence that he presented, words and emotions that are directed at water droplets before they are frozen have a profound effect on water crystals and the images they form, which can be either beautiful or ugly depending on the positive or negative nature of the energy addressed at them. Granted that the results of his research are accurate, if water responds physically to human speech and thoughts, it most certainly ought to react to human actions as well. That being the case, the images they must form in the oceans, rivers, lakes, and all bodies of water on the planet, are likely the most hideous representations of destruction. Considering the deplorable state of pollution in the vast bodies of water on the planet, I can only surmise that it must not be a sight for the faint of heart.

Horrific water crystals images aside, the problem that I create with my profit-seeking industrial production is the continuous contamination of a vital resource that is becoming more and more scarce as populations and urban centers continuously expand—and it's even worse in poverty-stricken nations. Incidentally, 46% of people on earth do not have water piped to their homes. Meanwhile, citizens of the wealthiest nation on the planet consume about 100 gallons of water at home daily, in contrast with millions of the world's poorest who subsist on fewer than five gallons a day. And with approximately 83 million more people who are added to the population tally each day, water demands will only keep going up. Soon, billions of people will live in regions where potable water is extremely scarce, which could lead to mass exodus, tension, violence, and wars motivated by lack of a natural resource that is impera- tive for survival. Lo rain shall become the new gold.

As the engineering machinery of Industrial Capi- talism recognizes the gravity of shortage of water, my scientific minions devote considerable amount of time and financial resources searching for supplies of water in outer space. It's well-known that the earth isn't the only place in the solar system with water. However, while water exists on earth because of its atmosphere that keeps liquid from floating away or being disinte- grated by solar radiation, elsewhere in the solar system it is present mostly as ice. The more scientists learn about how and where water survives, the more they understand how precious this resource is on their own home planet. I often marvel in disbelief at how they think of themselves as totally independent creatures from the earth; as if they could survive in another far away region of the cosmos on their own terms. Most likely, they'd soon introduce Industrial Capitalism so I can consume the newfound lands into oblivion like I've been doing to the planet earth.

As they search for water in outer space aware that this vital finite resource has been rapidly dwindling, they continue wasting it as if umpteen bottomless wells of fresh water were at their disposal. Golf courses, for instance, the recreational practice of mostly those who stand on the top of my economic system pyramid, requires an inordinate amount of water to maintain. In order to keep the fairways in good playing conditions, a staggering 2 billion gallons of water a day are used for golf courses irrigation in the United States alone.

Well, there is nothing to fret about. After all, advanced technology is already recycling waste water in large urban centers and turning it into "clean" drinking water for their thirsty populations. Besides, the inherent ingenuity of my selfish interest motive and profit-seeking economic activities has introduced the very lucrative commercialization of bottled drinking water. This business initiative—and socially acceptable commercial scam—aims at adding immediate profit and long-term value to the stocks of corporations running the bottled water operations. It should be a matter of time when canisters of quality breathing air become available for desperate consumers in high density metropolises. My lackeys always seem to find a way to make a profit out of the unfavorable conditions that my system creates.

As I demand continuous and endless production for the sake of consumption and survival, the ever sought-after profit comes with a hefty price tag; an ecological tariff that must be paid with injurious interest for the advantages obtained. Like the banks that rule over the operations of my system, the interests accrued in the taxing of the ecosystem are accumulated through a long-term process—think of a mortgage in which the longer the installment payments, the higher the interest collected by the financial institution. Thus, in my Industrial Capitalism system, which relies on ceaseless economic expansion for its survival, the cost of growth is charged to the ecological system account. Unfortunately, the already indebted ecosystem cannot survive when heavily taxed. The accumulating interest of ruin can be witnessed everywhere—and water has been paying a costly toll.

In order to feed an ever-growing population of servants and slaves of my system—and everyone must serve my needs, for their survival depends on mine—agricultural development is paramount. Although the idea of pollution often evokes images of billowing smokes spewing out of the filthy craters of industrial complexes, when it comes to water contamination the damage delivered through agricultural practices, though invisible to the naked eye, is as devastating as the harm done by industry and suburban development. But since the very important agricultural industry produces a commodity that is second only to availability of drinking water, mass-production of food supply is the greatest priority within my system. Ironically, it's also a primary source of water pollution.

There are several sub-industries within the broad agricultural industry: the produce industry, the poultry industry, the cattle industry, among many others. My system has managed to turn even animals into raw materials in the production of essential consumer goods. Each segment of the agricultural industry contributes with enormous amount of contaminants that are drained into various bodies of water wreaking havoc to food chains and drinking water for hundreds of millions of people. Countless waterways and coastal estuaries, the ideal locations for industrial development, have been and continue to be permanently damaged with polluted runoff flowing from factories, industries, and agriculture. Consequently, a growing list of endangered species contaminated with PCB (Polychlorinated Biphenyls, a persistent organic pollutant with high toxicity level), and other lethal chemicals have been dying and declining rapidly. Meanwhile, human health is impaired by the consumption of fish and other crustaceans infected with a smorgasbord of hazardous chemicals. In some cases, the demise of entire waterways and coastal estuaries stand as a silent warning of what might become of industrial civilization.

There used to be a most beautiful bay where majestic mountains stood in the background in which the highest peak was called "the finger of God," for it pointed toward the ample blue sky of infinity. Its emerald-color water was dotted with lovely small tropical islands whose palm trees swayed in the afternoon breeze. It was a most favorite nursery spot for humpback whales that traveled thousands of miles just for the privilege of giving birth to their calves in this pristine natural site. It was a playground for dolphins that enlivened the region with their blissful presence and remarkable intelligence. There was an abundance of marine life and the bay's water offered a bountiful harvest of seafood capable of feeding generations of the original inhabitants of the area. It was a small piece of paradise on earth—and I killed it!

Guanabara Bay is dead! I turned it into a filthy odorous swamp where the only life form that thrives in this slough of death is bacteria from raw sewage that feed on the industrial waste drained into the bay. The factories, refineries, power plants, and urban infrastructures that support the economic development of Rio de Janeiro and its mother country transformed Guanabara Bay into a disgusting cesspool. If that weren't enough to decimate beautiful abundant life, petroleum shipping vessels occasionally engaged in the nefarious criminal practice of washing off holding-tanks of crude oil in the bay. This method of poisoning the environment by dumping crude oil in ocean waters sometimes is purposeful and other times accidental. Nevertheless, both happen more often than the environment can handle.

When the 986-foot oil tanker, *The Exxon Valdez*, departed from the Trans Alaska Pipeline at 9:12pm on March 23, 1989, no one knew that the voyage would end up as one of the most grotesque environmental accidents in history. Within less than three hours of setting sail, the tanker ran aground on Bligh Reef, Alaska, spilling approximately 11 million gallons of crude oil into an estimated 1,300 miles of hitherto unspoiled environment. The carcasses of more than 35,000 birds and 1,000 sea otters were found after the spill; but since most carcasses sink, these numbers represent a small fraction of the actual death toll. Some watchdog groups offered more realistic statistics: 250,000 seabirds, 2,800 sea otters, 300 harbor seals, 250 bald eagles, 22 orca whales, and billions of salmon and herring eggs. A couple of decades after the disaster, oil persists in the environment, and in some places, is nearly as toxic as it was the first weeks after the spill.

Since oil is the life blood fueling Industrial Capitalism—petroleum is the bone marrow of my system—searching, drilling, and transporting this black liquid gold is inescapable, and so are the accidents likely to occur from time to time. Hence, on April 20, 2010, an explosion followed by fire on a drilling site mismanaged by a petroleum corporation triggered another environmental catastrophe. Besides the 11 reported deaths and 17 injured workers, it is estimated that between 35,000 and 60,000 barrels of oil (a barrel contains 44 gallons) spilled into the Gulf of Mexico each day, which makes *The Exxon Valdez* fiasco fade in comparison. More than 400 species of animals were harmed or at risk. A sea area larger than 4,000 square miles was covered with oil slick from the rig explosion, delivering a heavy blow to the local tourism and seafood industry; particularly shrimp—and the region represents 75% of the United States shrimp production. And to aggravate the scope and impact of the environmental damage, in order to clean up the mess, more than 11,140,000 gallons of oil were burned releasing massive amounts of CO_2 into the atmosphere (one gallon of gasoline emits 19.4 pounds of CO_2.) With 30,000 additional oil wells in the region, it is a matter of time for another mishap to take place. There are opportunities galore to establish a new environmental disaster record; and the oil industry offers many possibilities.

THE BEAST

As water is the most important natural resource for the survival of humankind and all other organic life forms, petroleum is fundamental for the survival of Industrial Capitalism. And even though my cronies of science desperately search for other renewable sources of energy—they know that petroleum, like water, also is a finite natural resource—the black liquid gold still is indispensable to the functioning of my economic machinery. Though they continue searching for new energy sources, the main focus of attention is for the immediate need to discover the hidden oil wells deeply buried in the entrails of the earth. Thus, researching, discovering, and drilling new potential sites are the ultimate energy supply needs of my system, regardless of the environmental risks they may pose.

In the kingdom of Industrial Capitalism dictated by the rules of fossil fuel-driven machines, petroleum is king.

7

Its name derived from the Latin words *petra*, meaning rock, and *oleum*, meaning oil, petroleum is a hydrocarbon; an organic compound containing carbon and hydrogen. It is the most important natural resource of my Industrial Capitalism economic system. I could not survive a day without it running through my veins of production.

Formed from organic remains of plants and animals that settled to the bottom of ancient oceans some millions of years ago, petroleum, the treasured elixir of industrialization, is an indispensable component for the proper functioning of my operations. Since the first oil well was drilled in 1859, this invaluable black crude natural resource not only catapulted massive industrial production to a higher level, but also became a most profitable industry in and by itself. It was a matter of time for the fledgling industry to dominate the entire economic machinery and provide the bulk of the energy the world depends on. It became the *de facto* ruler of Industrial Capitalism, therefore turning me into a slave of my own system.

Indeed, I am enslaved to petroleum. I depend on it for all transportation needs, including the production of asphalt that paves the roads for the billions of motor vehicles that circulate around the globe—and the automobile is one of the most important articles of consumption that I produce. Petroleum is also the raw material for numerous petrochemicals that produce, plastic, wax, fertilizers, lubricants, and many other critical goods that sustain my system. In addition, it is fundamental in the production of electricity to power the cities and provide heating for homes and businesses. In fact, in my flagship nation, the United States of America, petroleum is responsible for approximately 40 percent of total energy, and a whopping 97 percent of all the fuel used for transportation.

Since I've mentioned the United States of America as the role model of my system, it is suitable to use it as a representative of the petroleum issue. This country also serves as an indicator of the consequences of the economic dependence on this diminishing finite natural resource.

In the early 1900's petroleum was almost negligible as a source of energy production in the United States. It accounted for merely 4.8% of total energy production. By the mid-1950's petroleum production had gained a 40% share of energy production and has continued to rise ever since. The reason for this substantial increase in a short period of time is directly related to combustion engines used for transportation and machinery in industrial production. In addition, petroleum was also becoming the most popular form of energy for heating in residential and commercial buildings, among other uses. With the eventual increase in the production of electricity to sustain large urban centers, the demand for petroleum increased geometrically.

By 1948 the consumption and dependence of the United States on oil had increased manifolds. The country could no longer fulfill its demand for oil; there-fore it became a major importer of the commodity and relying heavily on foreign suppliers. Soon it became evident that the health of the nation's economy was tightly linked to the marketplace price of oil. And since everything in my system is dictated by the sacred free market principle of supply and demand, the United States and the rest of the world fell to their knees when the first major oil crisis came about in 1973. It was at this time that the Organization of Oil Exporting Coun-tries (OPEC) realized how powerful it was in a world whose economic development depended on its monop-olized natural resource. As major political upheavals and confrontations involving nations allied with some of the OPEC nation-members, oil became more than just an invaluable commodity: it turned into a powerful political bargaining tool. Thus, because of the United States support to the nation of Israel during the Yom Kippur War in 1973, OPEC imposed an oil embargo that triggered escalating cost and shortage of gasoline prompting the country to ration this resource, which had a devastating consequence in its economy.

Some six years later, another major oil crisis emerged when a revolution in a country-member of OPEC happened in 1979. A bitter enemy of the United States, the Iranian Revolution caused ripple effects sim-ilar to the energy crisis of 1973. Then, in 1990, another energy crisis took place when Iraq, an OPEC nation-member, invaded its organization counterpart, Kuwait, setting off another oil crisis. Although the latter crisis was not as serious as the previous two, it revealed the vulnerability of the United States and the rest of the world's economy to their dependence on petroleum. It'd be a matter of time when another crisis would surface—and many others shall follow until oil supplies finally run out as the demand for it increases exponentially.

If economic and political conflicts were not enough to destabilize the oil industry, natural disasters can also have a profound impact on the supply and distribution of petroleum products everywhere, as it was evinced in 2005 with the potent hurricane that struck an oil rich area. Hurricane Katrina contributed to increasing the price of crude oil to unprecedented record. Then, there are thousands of miles of pipeline running through different regions of the world to supply oil to vital industrial and urban centers, some of which pass through earthquake-prone lands. If any geological disturbance were to happen that affected the delivery of crude oil to its destination, the socioeconomic and political repercussions would be incalculable—not to mention the potential for catastrophic accidents.

And as demand for oil increases so does the price of the barrel. Since many OPEC countries are opposed to the United States international policies and dominance in the world, they're likely to turn this trend into a major advantage in their conflict with the superpower nation. Consuming an average of 20 million barrels of oil per day—2 million barrels coming from an antagonist OPEC nation-member—the United States gobbles up approximately 26% of the world's oil, though its population is about 4.6% of the world's total. In fact, if the U.S. were to stop producing and importing oil, its reserves would not last longer than a month. If it stopped importing but continued internal production while accessing its strategic reserves, then the oil supply would last approximately 45 days. That is to say, any social, political, or economic turmoil in the world, particularly within OPEC country members, has the potential to deliver a serious blow to globalized economy and push the world into a dangerous crisis.

The experts monitoring the overall stability of my system stipulate that half of all recoverable oil reserves buried in the entrails of the earth has already been used up. If the world continues to consume at the current rate of 25 billion barrels per year—and the consumption rate will definitely increase as economies and populations expand—in another 50 years all crude oil on earth should run out completely.

The inference is obvious: without the black blood that runs through the veins of my system delivering the nutrients that keep me alive, I will not be able to survive; and if I don't, modern industrial civilization will come to an end as well. The irony is that I pose a catch-22 dilemma to humanity: they will perish if I continue to grow and they will face their demise if I stop growing. If I ever run out of energy, I'll collapse dragging them down with me. In a sense, the black blood that nurtures my entire system while undermining human health with its waste disposal is the "Black Plague of Industrial Capitalism." And like the black plague that decimated European societies in the Dark Ages, this one, too, is destined to blow the winds of death through the concrete jungles of industrial societies.

However, in the grand scope of mass production for profit that characterize my economic system, pollution is not limited to filthy smoke spewing out of factories and motor vehicles, or plastic bags and other petroleum derivatives that litter the oceans and taint the landfills. There are, indeed, many spin-offs of contamination resulting from the way of life that my existence imposes on human beings and their environment. But of all forms of pollution that I create by the very nature of my system, none is more damaging than the one that takes place within the human being himself.

Driven by the covetous pursuit of profit in unrestrained competition where everyone fights for his and her own self-interest, I manage to prostitute humanity by defiling the character and purpose of work in their lives. Since the yardstick with which to measure success is the amount of wealth an individual accumulates in his lifetime, they do anything—and crush anyone along the way—to achieve the ultimate elusive goal of prosperity. But there is a hefty price to pay for their shallow material dreams.

As they waste away their fleeting existence on earth, I enslave them with the daily drudgery and grind of unfulfilled labor, as they devote their wretched lives to my economic demands above anything else. The incessant work for the sake of unrestrained consumption alienates them from nature, their fellow-human beings, and worst of all, themselves. As they lose their connection with the fundamental meaning of life, they fall into silent desperation. Isolated within their own misery, they resort to reconnect with themselves and others through addicting technological trinkets.

They are doomed!

8

The first victim to succumb to my economic system's implacable methods was one of the most important aspects of human life: work; the severance of man from his work to be precise. This is not to say that human labor wasn't already limping along the tortuous—and torturous—course of history before I came into being. However, once the philosophical foundation of my intellectual progenitor, Adam Smith, was solidly established following the Industrial Revolution, I stripped the individual from his work and turned it into a quantifiable commodity; the palpable energy of Capital. I transformed work into job.

Of all human activities work is arguably the most important one. It is the main pillar buttressing the individual's identity in the world and a fundamental source of creativity, pride, and personal fulfillment. It bestows upon citizens the value of their contributions to the welfare of the community they belong; and this is deeply rooted in men's psyche from primordial tribal time. By its intrinsic nature, work imbues a sense of dignity, honor, and self-respect in the human person. Like bees out in the meadows, it is through his work that a man extracts the nectar that sweetens his life. Conversely, there is the bitterness in the labor of a job.

There is a distinct difference between work and labor. The former is an expression of one's identity and contribution to society, while the latter is the economic function one carries out in the doing of a job in order to make a living. This concept of labor was developed in the mid-18th century by the ingenuity of my creator and distorted in the following century by the ingenuousness of my archrival and mortal enemy. This man, who is an adamant adversary of the selfish rights of the individual over the welfare of society and whose name I refuse to utter, introduced his labor theory of value in which he proposes the concept of surplus value (the value extracted from the commodity labor-power purchased for less than it is worth, the exchange-value of labor, which becomes capital). Thus, the owners of the means of production build up their wealth through the labor of their workers, just as the landlords profited from the labor of their serfs and the slave owner from his human property. Therefore, according to this enemy of individual prosperity, Capital is but accumulated labor.

The mechanization brought about by the Industrial Revolution validated the concept of accumulated labor as Capital even before the theory was conceived. By instituting division of labor as a fundamental component of efficiency in industrial production, profits increased exponentially as more goods were produced in shorter periods of time. Division of labor allowed breaking down the production process into as many simple and repetitive functions as possible in order to minimize time-consuming skills and judgment. The immediate result was improved productivity, but the direct consequence was the degradation of work from a personal creative act and source of pride to a tedious chore that turned daily life into miserable drudgery. It was the first step toward alienating man from himself.

By the end of the 19th century when industrial output was reaching unprecedented levels, sophisticated techniques for adulterating the functions of labor exacerbated the alienation of workers even further. In order to increase production—and profits—a new systematic approach to management was introduced and became known as "scientific management." Although there is nothing really scientific about it, its creator, Frederick W. Taylor, was convinced that each worker's particular abilities could be scientifically manipulated with the ultimate objective of establishing managerial control of the production process. The trick was to assign the right employees to the right jobs that they would do in repetitive fashion, while large planning departments coordinated and monitored each detail in the production process. Taylorism, as the practice became known, was a great economic success and reflected the era's love affair with the idea of efficiency. The human cost for this managerial system was an increase disconnect of the individual worker from his labor.

The human labor situation was significantly aggravated when Taylorism, which had been welcomed with great enthusiasm by industrialists, merged with an equally resourceful approach to increasing industrial production: the assembly line. Although Henry Ford was not the first one to introduce this innovative technology, he's certainly improved it with the massive output of affordable motor vehicles, which became known as Fordism. In his assembly line, he reversed the process of automobile manufacturing production;

that is, instead of workers going to the car, the car came to the workers who performed the same task of assembly over and over again. Thus, the combination of scientific management and Ford's production system became the twin beacons guiding the captains of industry and their massive industrial motherships toward an auspicious new century that promised unprecedented economic and technological advancement.

And so the promising 20th century is heralded as the fastest growing development time in human history. An era that began with wagons powered by horses would close with spacecrafts fueled by nuclear energy; from bicycles to airplanes; and from the telegraph to the World Wide Web. Marked by such extraordinary progress in a mere one hundred years, no wonder they worship my Industrial Capitalism as a God-given inspiration to humankind. But the delusional blessing came in tandem with a horrific curse; the curse of human alienation and decimation of the natural environment.

By the time World War I broke out in 1914, it became evident that neglecting the fundamental needs and rights of peoples and nations would have disastrous consequences in the future. Nevertheless, they've been ignoring the many writings on the wall that warn them of the portentous effects engendered by their social irresponsibility. To the contrary, they revere the inhumane way of life that my economic system imposes on them, and they proudly accept it as a morally ordained social order.

Underneath the opulence generated by my economic system lies the oppressed and alienated human being. The nature of my system demands that instead of relating to one another cooperatively, they must foster a competitive culture in which they constantly try to out-do their fellowmen by all possible means. Love and trust are replaced by bargaining and exchange. I strictly command that they cease to recognize in one another their common human nature. Instead, they must see others either as unwelcome competitors who must be eliminated, or as opportune instruments for furthering their own egoistic interests. As they serve the needs of my economic system, their work activity must be impersonal and a disconnected function of their beings, which they dread but cannot escape. I mislead them into believing that they're in charge of their work, but at the same time I force them to sell their cheap labor in a crowded and highly competitive job marketplace. Meanwhile, a small number of my privileged lackeys will use their own and owned labor to accumulate even more Capital.

Hence, I've managed to transform what once was the individual's fundamental life-activity into a market-regulated commodity that the worker must sell in order to survive—and often times the earnings are not even enough for their survival needs. I have no qualms in acknowledging that my economic system has turned one of the most important aspects of human life into a mere means of eking out a living; that work is no longer a part of a man's life, but a sacrifice of his life. His real life begins only when his work ceases. And since he spends most of his time "on the job," he becomes dissatisfied with his life as depression, anxiety, and anger take over and rule the experience of his slavish existence.

There is no need to fret, though. My system assuages the trepidations that stir internal conflicts in the disgruntled human being with an array of palliatives. Firstly, it's important to maintain a very busy schedule that leaves no time to worry or interest in meaningful critical thinking. Equally important is to have widespread availability of fatuous entertainment and constant bombardment of information, many of which is fear-inducing data that keeps me in total control of the apprehensive populations. Fear of the wrath of God, unemployment, bankruptcy, terrorism, disease, death; whatever the source may be, fear is my most potent weapon of subordination.

And if ignorance is bliss, as the popular adage purports, then I've delivered the masses back to the Garden of Eden.

9

As the twentieth century progressed and technology evolved at an unprecedented rate, it became much easier to manipulate and control the working herd. After confining the human cattle to cubicles that resemble corrals where they toil brainlessly like oxen plowing a barren field of bureaucracy, I turned the work of the upper level functions to the same degree of drudgery of their factory slave labor counterparts. I managed to level both the blue and the white-collar workers to similar standards of mediocrity. Day in and day out, they glare at computer screens entering and collecting data that adds absolutely nothing to their personal pride and creativity in a production process that is utterly disconnected from their lives—and they do it while bombarded by EMF (electromagnetic field) radiation. In due time, the senseless repetitive tasks deflate their spirit, corrodes their mental capacity, and alienate them from a meaningful human experience. They become the walking dead whose respite can only be found in inane entertainment, electronic stimulation, shopping, and varied forms of addictions. Alas, many succumb to depression and despair in the agony of an empty and meaningless existence.

In spite of the increasing frustrations with the daily grind of their work lives, they must continue toiling away with a false sense of contentment. It is as though they sailed against the wind while queasy and daunted by the constant oscillation of the market. In the prime of their productive time, they fasten the feeble security harness of their jobs; and as they get older, they hold on to the flagging ropes of their life's savings with a shaky fearful grip. Jumping overboard is a very hazardous endeavor, for they'd have to swim in the deep sea of unemployment and risk drowning in the frostbiting cold water of poverty. And no matter how nauseated they are, they must stay onboard and obey the captains of industry and their numerous obedient sailors who navigate through tempestuous waters toward a distant imaginary fantasy island of prosperity. However, the disposable deckhands will be forced to walk the plank of lay-off and fall into unemployment any time the captains determine that their profits are threatened by the competition of faster sailing corporate ships.

The empty lives of workers sway along with the motions of the market that determines what directions they ought to follow. Overworked, deprived of free time, stressed, frightened, and unable to establish meaningful relationships with the self, others, and nature, they resort to the wonders of the electronic age as a desperately needed distraction from their existential misery. Thus, they join social networks on the internet—a misnomer since my system has turned the fad into profitable commercial networks—texting, viewing, tweeting, among other distracting activities that only solidifies my stronghold on passive and alienated individuals who have lost interest in anything outside the frivolous experience of their empty lives. Lo the masses are absolutely contemptible!

My minions must be constantly busy. Either they're gawking at computer monitors all day doing insipid repetitive work; or watching brain dwarfing television shows that short-circuits critical thinking; or babbling along on cell phones not learning about the value of solitude; or text-messaging uninterruptedly anyone, anytime, and for no reason other than disconnecting further from their unbearable reality; or following the irrelevant lives of my market-produced celebrities on frivolous communication devices; or developing cyber relationships with people they've never had eye contact with; or shutting themselves off from their surroundings plugged in to earphones; or playing violent video games that desensitize their human ability to feel compassion and empathy; or whatever other means they choose is alright by me. As long as they're disconnected from critical thinking and do not rebel against my way of carrying out my business, I'll be able to smother any threat to my dominance in the world.

I definitely want to be acknowledged with reverence and praise for the outstanding plan of action I put in place. In order to secure such an impeccable slavery system, it's been paramount to set off the process at the embryonic stage of the slave class. Like the fiction work of writer Aldous Huxley in which an artificial society is methodically programmed to be content, I, too, have applied an approach that is even more validating than the fictional slant of a literary work. In his novel *Brave New World*, Huxley portrays a congruous class society whose citizens are born in human laboratories where genetic engineering, mind-conditioning, and drug-induced emotional states establish a perfectly harmonious society, albeit artificial, in which all citizens are satisfied with their social status. But unlike the science-fiction twist of an imaginary social reality, my system has managed to establish such a society within the parameters of morally acceptable conditions that are defended to the death even by the lowest ranking members of the social strata. By comparison, Huxley's superb literary talent is unmatched against the geniality of my capacity to manipulate the masses; not only in subtle imperceptibility but also in socially acceptable fashion. I am so proud of my achievements that I want to detail my Machiavellian strategy.

It all begins with the establishment of a poignant culture solidly based on sacrosanct principles: liberty, justice for all, freedom—the latter is deeply entwined with the concept of free market economics—nationalism, pride, honor, morality, and, of course, God. In this fashion, the social culture of domination becomes a bona fide religion that my followers worship and willingly sacrifice their lives for its honorable existence. Soon, independent thinking, personal beliefs, and common sense are alchemized into a collective blind faith guided by fervent patriotic emotions. Then, they surrender their individuality to an authoritative mindset that thinks and acts in their behalf without their even noticing it. My strategy is so wickedly brilliant that even I astound myself with my accomplishments. Only the Christian Church methodology of manipulation has surpassed the efficiency of my approach for exercising control over the masses. Germany's Third Reich is worthy of acknowledgement as well.

The next step is to inculcate the values of the culture through uninterrupted propaganda until they become deeply ingrained in the collective identity of a nation. Joseph Goebbels, the Minister of Public Enlightenment and Propaganda of the Third Reich, was a virtuoso propagandist whose exceptional implementation of a captivating nationalistic strategy brought an entire nation to uncompromising servitude. Aware that the masses are absolutely contemptible and indifferent to interests outside their immediate experience, he bombarded the airwaves, media, and all available means of communication opportunities to promote the proud values of the Germanic race and culture. Once he impregnated the nation with the semen of nationalism, he fathered a new consciousness of obedience while constricting the citizens to surrender their will to the control of the Third Reich. Goebbels believed that the behavior of the masses was determined, not by knowledge and reason, but by feeling and unconscious drives. It is through these drives and feelings that attitudes for controlled behaviors are implanted by the propagandist who can then manipulate these instincts and emotions at will. This approach is particularly favorable when the masses are bewildered, frustrated, and chronically ridden with anxiety.

The ominous image of a humungous nuclear mushroom cloud marks the end of the Goebbels propaganda era. But once the radioactive dust settled down on the barren cities of Hiroshima and Nagasaki, a new and powerful propaganda machinery empire emerged to become second only to the formidable brainwashing strategies of the Christian Church: the American Empire.

Although I could make a case about the former Soviet Union, which emerged as the nemesis of the American Empire at the beginning of the Nuclear Age, it's not worth mentioning because the Soviet Union's control over the masses was mostly imposed by sheer force and oppression. Besides, from an analytical standpoint I could argue that their indoctrination strategy was actually counter-productive, for it greatly benefited my economic and political system while bestowing upon the communist bloc an unscrupulous reputation. No wonder the Soviet Union tumbled down in a domino effect of self-defeat.

On the other hand, the American Empire is the Mecca of free enterprise; the international inspiration of *laissez-faire* Capitalism; the pantheon where the noble concepts of liberty, freedom, and justice for all reigns as the sacred dictum that a God fearing people blindly accept as undeniable truth. In order to sustain such a high level of widespread devotion in a social scenario that blatantly denies the veracity of eloquent words, an immaculately effective propaganda system must be in place—and they play it like a magical fiddle that bewitches the hoi polloi with patriotic fervor and maudlin religiosity.

Coincidentally or not, there are several similarities between Goebbels's Third Reich propaganda strategies and the American Empire methods. Most strikingly, is their mutual appeal to patriotism while fomenting nationalistic fever that is ubiquitous in society and present in a variety of cultural, athletic, and other events where massive gatherings take place. Mass psychology suggests that when people are assembled in a crowd, their individual identity is lost in the collective emotions of the group, which leaves them highly susceptible to increased suggestibility and they cease to having discernible judgment of their own. They may become very excitable and lose all sense of individual or collective responsibility. They may act as though they were under the influence of a potent drug that alters their state of mind. They become prime targets for "herd intoxication." It is in such vulnerable conditions that the opportunity to inject the masses with potent doses of fervent patriotism presents itself. It is the perfect occasion to hail nationalistic values and the glories of the economic and political system it represents, which is exemplified in the reverence to the national symbol.

Pledging allegiance to a national flag, for instance, is not only an oath of loyalty to the country it represents, but also to the socioeconomic and political values it stands for. The infusion of patriotic passion delivered by this persuasive ritualistic act is immeasurable. Aware of this important component of nationalistic propaganda, Francis Bellamy wrote in 1892 what he termed The Pledge of Allegiance, which has been modified four times since then, with the most recent change introducing the words "under God" in 1954. The latest edition added a powerful religious element to maximize its effect on a predominantly Christian society. The current version reads: "I pledge allegiance to the flag of the United States of America, and the republic for which it stands, one nation under God, indivisible, with

[66]

liberty and justice for all." Without grasping the empirical meaning of an "indivisible nation with liberty and
justice for all," the citizens under the influence of the
patriotic fix surrender the very liberty and sense of
equalitarian justice in their deeply divided nation. Thus,
they recite the Pledge of Allegiance in rote mode fashion with the same absence of being they carry out their
uninteresting daily activities. And this is what works
best for the preservation of my economic system's interests, especially when the pledge is sworn by innocent children in the public school system.

No propaganda strategy can become effective
without a solid educational system in place to promote
its values. Every social, economic, political, and religious institution has been aware of this fundamental
necessity. As it happens in Huxley's fictional *Brave
New World* society, they know the importance of mind-
conditioning children to think, act, and behave according to the dominant social order. As they grow up im-
bued with the values they were trained to accept as
morally legitimate, they become obedient servants of
the system; much like the religious fundamentalist who
sacrifices his life for the honorable cause of defending
what he believes to be true. Hence, children are methodically conditioned to believe from a very early age
that they live in freedom. And yet, the freedom of
childhood—the most carefree phase of the human experience—is usurped from their fledgling lives for the
sake of preparation to fulfill an economic function in
the distant future. The creative, imaginative, and play-
ful kindergarten experience has been replaced by a rig-
orous academic training. The well-being of my eco-

nomic system demands it to be this way; and so does their individual needs to succeed—make more money, that is—in the ever-growing competitive job market. Lo these loathsome creatures feed me with their own lives. I say death to childhood! Long live Capitalism!

As they grow older, they are broken into the delusion that there is real liberty and justice for all. However, the blatant inequalities and indifferences to the underprivileged kids in the school-yard do not go unnoticed. By the time they get to high school, they are led to accept democracy as the only honorable political system in the world. But soon they scratch their heads in confusion when they find out that other countries are invaded when the results of their democratic elections do not meet my international economic needs. In order to reinforce my values, my propaganda machinery perjures them to believe that their dominant country is the paragon of virtues, until they learn about the theft of lands and atrocities committed against native peoples. And yes, they learn that all of this happens in the indivisible nation under God. But when they go to Church on Sunday morning, they are forgiven for having learned so much about hypocrisy, as long as they promise not to question or rebel against the rules I dictate to the world.

What is truly fascinating is that in spite of all the contradictions and incongruities inherent in my socio-economic political system, it not only works but I'm also invigorated with the passing of time. I attribute the exceptional success of the unquestioned acceptance of my dominance to my highly sophisticated propaganda and mind-conditioning systems, which begin in the very early stages of the educational system. It becomes more challenging when children start growing and exploring their inhered intellectual inquisitiveness, for that is the time some of them may break away. This is the time when the defense mechanisms of my system are launched to safeguard its survival. Through the vast and ever-expanding mass-communication systems available to me by the rapid development of technology, I am able to reinforce the misinformation of my system continuously, therefore cementing the mind-conditioning children receive throughout the early stages of their upbringing. The message is reiterated daily on corporate controlled television, radio, the motion-picture industry, on the Web, and on all sorts of handheld devices. It happens round the clock and everywhere. My message is continuous and ubiquitous. In fact, it's nearly impossible to escape the bombardment of information that conveys one fundamental concept: I am the best system money can buy.

There are many steps leading to the top of the pyramid where the mirage of the precious stone beacons its titillating appeal. Even the downtrodden is enticed to believe that they, too, can climb up and claim the jewel of financial freedom for themselves. As they sacrifice the quality of their lives for a prize that already has been snatched by the invisible hand of a small percentage of my servants, they die without even noticing that they were nothing but slaves who helped building the pyramid of the pharaohs of Capitalism.

As for the vast majority of people who lack the wherewithal, both my supporters and I despise their insignificant existence. We consider them losers. However, I hold a modicum of gratitude to the proletariat, for I'm aware that without their cheap labor and mass consumption of gaudy goods I wouldn't be able to thrive as well as I do. They are well domesticated and obedient subordinates of my system.

But regardless of individual economic status, there is fairness in my system that establishes a common denominator that renders everyone as docile as a pussy cat: FEAR!

10

Fear has the potential to impact the human psyche in a similar way the atomic bomb can have on the physical environment: total devastation.

Fear gives birth to anxiety, the self-defeating anticipatory thought about something that might never happen in the future. And yet, the nature of this negative emotion triggers an illusory experience in the present moment as if the dreadful thought were real. This distorted focused attention generates a pessimistic feeling that paves the way to an emotional swamp where the individual waddles through helplessly. Therefore, it should not come as a surprise that cultivation of fear is arguably the most powerful tool in my arsenal for the control and manipulation of the masses. It is the whip with which I flog my slave herd to submit to my commands, while intimidating them not to dare to stray from the pack. In the complex nuances of my being, fear is the hub to which all the spokes of life are connected.

In my economic system ruled by greed and the selfish pursuit of profit in which the winner takes it all, the most prevalent cause of anxiety among the competitors, regardless of their monetary ranking in the competition game, is the fear of losing economic ground—and worse yet, destitution. Those who have accumulated extraordinary riches by depriving their fellow-citizens from their fair share of the national wealth, they fear losing a lifestyle of luxury they grew accustomed to enjoying. Conversely, the populous majority who toil for slave wage at the bottom of the pile of profit, they are tormented daily with the looming prospect of getting laid-off, getting sick, or any other means of losing their survival income. Even the passing thought of losing their jobs can make them weak in the knees. And since my system offers absolutely no guarantees that the worker will retain his ability to provide for his family, the fear of losing his employment drives him to work harder for even less compensation. Yet, they can be dismissed unceremoniously at any time the employer deems necessary for the increased profitability of the business. After all, the selfish pursuit of profit is the cardinal rule of my economic dictum and it must be observed accordingly. Besides, labor is but disposable commodity.

The geniality—and irony—of this trepidation roller-coaster is that the same fear that terrifies the masses of wage slave workers of losing their livelihood is the same that haunts the wealthy of losing or diminishing their loot. Thus, the fear itself perpetuates a vicious cycle of lay-offs and unemployment because corporations export jobs in order to sustain or increase the lucrative status of shareholders portfolios. But again, labor is but a cheap supply for my demands—and my ultimate demand is more profit.

Although the players on the opposing ends of the rope of Capitalism's tug of war feel the tension of the pull, the rope always ruptures at its weakest place; and when it does, a multitude falls into poverty. The ones in the middle of the class game are just dragged down while desperately holding on to splitting threads of the rope still in their hands. And since my economic system is driven by fierce competition in the pursuit of self-interest, the mode of cooperation is non-existent and undesirable because it's contradictory to my principles, which leaves the fallen players in dire straits. I want to be clear that my system does not tolerate any suggestions insinuating the introduction of a cooperative economic approach to the iniquitous competitive game. My lackeys are sure to cry foul and accuse the proponents of cooperative economic measures as the enemies of freedom, liberty, and justice for all. But what they actually mean is that those utopian humanitarians are against inhumane free market practices, liberty to unbridled accumulation in detriment to the welfare of others, and justice for the rights of those who own it all. Lo I hail my fury against those idealist progressive thinkers who are the dangerous enemies of my freedom; the inalienable rights of the free market.

Trampled by unfair competition and smashed by the greed of powerful business interests, the average wage worker lives in a state of pending panic. Not only they fret about unexpected unemployment, but also they have to compete against the very energy that fuels my entire system: Capital. Meanwhile, corporations—the mighty economic entities to which the invisible hand of the market is attached to—have been ruled by the highest court of law to have the same rights as those of individual citizens of the United States of America. This ruling has legitimized my existence as a bona fide impersonal living entity that unofficially governs the world. But for those men and women who depend exclusively on the fruits of their labor to survive and support loved ones, the terror of impoverishment, like the shadow of death, walks by their side through the course of a lifetime. Thus, poverty becomes the Sword of Damocles hanging by a single hair of a horse's tail over the head of the most vulnerable citizens.

In the end, it is all about financial success, which is the ultimate reward for the business gladiators who vanquish their competitors in the free market coliseum. Conversely, poverty is the ultimate punishment for those hurled into the competitive arena where they must fight for survival against ferocious contenders with insatiable appetite for lucrative deals. In either case, the fear of succumbing to destitution produces unbearable anxiety to countless people, and that leads to a concatenation of social and physical ailments. But regardless of the circumstances, my system amasses an inordinate amount of profit from them all!

Lost in the reveries of their tenuous economic dreams—the flagship nation of my system cleverly relates to it as "the American dream"—an inordinate number of people are abruptly awakened to the reality of experiencing financial nightmares. In the habitual economic cycle of boom and bust that characterizes Capitalism, people constantly worry about the prospect of losing their jobs, livelihood, homes, and even their self-esteem. Constantly worried about remaining afloat in a sea of economic uncertainty, health related consequences affect both the physical and the mental aspects of their lives. What follows then is a medley of potential illnesses for every personality type: mental health breakdown leading to chronic depression; excessive alcohol consumption as escapism; domestic violence triggered by emotional disturbances aggravated by financial stress; drugs, sex, and food addictions; inane mind-numbing forms of entertainment; and, of course, all sorts of electronic distractions to keep my servants alienated from the abusive nature of my system. And by the way, do I need to point out that there are opportunities for profit galore in every concocted, reactive, or legitimate illness I'm committed to fostering?

However, this sociological backlash is not limited to those on the bottom of the economic oppression pile; it applies to every slave worker shackled by the tight grip of a job his life depends on. Either they have too much money or none at all; are obscenely compensated or abusively underpaid; are the oppressors or the oppressed; they all end up as potential victims of physical and mental illnesses. As they profit in cash they must also pay with their health—and even more so for their health care.

Being fear an invaluable stimulant for profitable economic activities—and human health an indispensable element for quality life—sickness naturally becomes a treasured commodity for building wealth in my economic system. Like food and water, humans cannot live long and well without good health. They must nurture it, maintain it, and take care of its needs whenever an emergency arises, lest the consequences may sometimes be fatal. Thus, aware of the absolute necessity of health care, I turned it into a most profitable Capitalistic venture; a multi-billion dollar industry that enriches a handful of my lackeys.

For the millions of people who cannot afford this vital commodity service, I express my feigned regrets and disingenuous condolences. To the rest of privileged consumers stimulating this vigorous industry of mine, I greet you with heartfelt enthusiasm: welcome to the sick business of health care.

11

In order to ensure that my underlings conform to the demands of my system without rebelling against the ruthless servitude I impose on them, I keep all my worker-slaves on a daily mental diet of distractions and futilities that entertain their hollow minds when they are not occupied with the drudgeries of labor. As for the physical body, I supply tantalizing palate pleasures stimulated by aggressive advertising campaigns promoting high fat and sugary processed foods. The combination of insalubrious eating habits and overbearing everyday stress establishes the foundation for building a very profitable commercial enterprise. Thus, as they become physically vulnerable and emotionally moribund, they capitulate to all sorts of illnesses that my economic system cashes in big time through the sick business of health care.

Considering the endless possibilities for profits this commodity can generate in the booming health care industry, it is obvious that not-so-hidden forces within my system ensure that this critical human service remains a lucrative tradable stock on the market. Furthermore, it compels employees to remain bound to their workplace for fear of losing access to a literally vital service that can be unaffordable if acquired on their own. In fact, for low-wage workers, even with health insurance in place, the cost of medical care can be exorbitant. Since health is indispensable to quality of life, health care is a necessary commodity that people must have, lest they shall face grave consequences; not only health related but also financial ruin. After all, the obscene free market value of this product service is a most profitable commodity in the multibillion dollar industry of sickness.

Although common sense and social morality have tried to meddle in the health care business segment of my system, the industry has been able to distort the interpretation of ethical concepts, such as human rights. After the worldwide catastrophe brought about by the war that inaugurated the nuclear age, the nations of the world assembled together on December 10, 1948 to proclaim the Universal Declaration of Human Rights. Article 25 (1) of this document reads:

> Everyone has the right to a standard of living adequate for the health and well-being of himself and his family, including food, clothing, housing and medical care and necessary social services, and the right to security in the event of unemployment, sickness, disability, widowhood, old age or other lack of livelihood in circumstances beyond his control.

Even though the document specifically states that health, well-being, and medical care are to be considered inviolable human right, this is not the case in many of the undersigned countries, including the wealthiest nation on earth where health care is an ever-expanding lucrative industry. Consequently, the cost of

this commodity service skyrockets continuously as determined by market forces under the consecrated tenets
of supply and demand and the pursuit of profit.

Indeed, the quality of medical care in the affluent
United States is arguably the best in the world. Unfortunately, it is available only for the very few privileged
citizens who can afford the luxury of excellent services.
Having the best health care system in the world is tantamount to having the best hotels in the world in which
only a selected clientele can check in. For the millions
of people whose pecuniary situation turns medical care
into an inaccessible indispensable service, the price-tag
of a healthy life is out of their consumer range. Consequently, millions of people in the wealthiest nation in
the world have absolutely no access to health care,
some of whom struggle with debilitating illnesses. Besides their health woes, they totter on the fringe of financial bankruptcy.

The radical critics of my economic system come
up in arms claiming that not having universal health
care is a travesty and a blatant violation of human
rights; at least according to the international covenant
established by the United Nations. Those intellectual
and humanitarian troublemakers attempt to confront
and reject two fundamental principles of my economic
system that bestows extraordinary wealth for nations,
albeit in the controlling hands of just a few citizens.
These principles are the pursuit of profit in *laissez-faire*
style—the lifeblood of Capitalism—and individual interests superseding the common welfare of the entire
population of contributing citizens. The health care industry is an important component of free enterprise,

[79]

and the participants in this industry have their own interests in mind. They are supporting my system in most traditional fashion. As for the deplorable mob of free-thinkers who portray the health care industry as a human right-bequeathing institution, it would behoove them to be grateful that this valuable commodity is available in the free marketplace, which is even offered to many duly employed workers. The only difference is that what they consider to be a human right, my economic system calls it a benefit.

Of course for those who do not have the benefit of health insurance, either because they are out of work, self-employed, or simply cannot keep up with the escalating cost of health care policies, their financial situation can get quickly compromised if a health issue comes up. Some extremists make use of vitriolic arguments to discredit my system, claiming that low-income people should not have to choose between putting food on the table and exhausting their financial resources with health care. They offer case after case of countless middle-class individuals and families who file for bankruptcy after having to finance the cost of health care related issues. The afflicted have to sell their homes and personal belongings, drain their savings and retirement accounts, and apply for high-interest loans and credit plans from greedy financial institutions. In the end, after their lives are ravaged by debt, their credit ratings plunge and so does their ability to find work to pay for what they owe—having acceptable credit scores as a requisite for obtaining employment is another brilliant entrapment strategy to keep people obligated to my modus operandi.

THE BEAST

I understand and acknowledge that individual financial crisis is a leading cause of health related issues. However, to be fair for a change, it can happen to anyone gambling in my casino-like economic system, regardless of how many chips he has stacked up on the table. That's the nature of The Beast: the pursuit of profit is fraught with dangers of losses. Thus, the unwavering pressure to produce income, along with the hovering fear of losing a job (the means of making a living) or depreciation of Capital investments (the idle source of generating passive earnings) can lead a man to the brink of desperation. The unforgiving anxiety has its toll in manifold facets of human health, which is particularly manifested in the mounting cases of mental illnesses diagnosis across all levels of economic strata of the population. I'm the one who drives them mad.

Besides the evident symptoms of excessive stress on the physical body (high blood pressure, coronary diseases, ulcers, etc.), depression runs rampant in modern industrial societies. In fact, because the pressure to perform, compete, and succeed in an increasingly competitive job market starts at the very early stages of human development, the number of children exhibiting the symptoms of depression is growing at alarming rates. And as the number of acronyms to describe these juvenile mental illnesses augment, so does the variety of drugs available in the obscenely profitable pharmaceutical industry—an essential offshoot of the health care industry—to assuage the pseudo-pathological plague of children; not to mention minimizing the emotional burden of the teachers and parents who have to interact with them.

It is highly probable that these mental disturbances are triggered by the radical change in social environment where children are pressured to perform at a very young age. While they are compelled to forsake the innocent years of the precious gift of childhood, scientists serving the interests of profit-seeking drug companies work hard on specious researches sponsored by the pharmaceutical industry. The dubious results are as expected: mental illnesses are due to biochemical imbalance, genetic heritage, among other possibilities that psychotropic medications can manage or even cure. Suddenly, a miracle drug is developed in the same laboratories where the scientific research was conducted. After hastened evaluations by the agency that is supposed to oversee the safety of medications—and whose many board members have conflict of interest with the pharmaceutical industry—the new wonder drug is introduced on the market followed by massive advertising campaign. It is no accident that antidepressants are among the most prescribed drugs in the United States. Thus, profits soar and wealthy stock holders temporarily forget about their own mental breakdowns.

Although history abounds with evidences of mentally and emotionally disturbed individuals, the number and types of disorders have increased exponentially since the beginning of the twentieth century. Surely, some mental illnesses may very well be caused by chemical imbalance or genetic heritage, but there is a plethora of evidence that the vast majority of mental disorders in modern society are caused by socioeconomic pressures; psychological illnesses created by severe sociological dysfunction. Isn't it fascinating?

THE BEAST

My economic system creates the circumstances for the escalation of mental illnesses and at the same time establishes the consumer base for a multi-billion dollar industry to thrive. That's the ingenuity of Capitalism—and its utmost disregard for human welfare. But that is the nature of The Beast; the essence of who I am.

It is no wonder that giant pharmaceutical companies have become the new darlings of big business in the wonderful world of Capitalism. They have seized control of the ancient and dying practice of healing by switching the focus from medicine to marketing. First off, they invent diseases to be investigated and authenticated by bogus scientific researches before coming up with a miracle pill that will cure the concocted maladies. Then, they diplomatically bribe doctors into prescribing the new expensive product to sickened consumers of health care goods. The legal drug cartels headquartering in Wall Street cajole their pushers by giving away all sorts of incentives, ranging from luxury international vacations to a handful of good old cash. But more importantly, they inundate media outlets with enticing advertisement that caters to fears and hopes of the afflicted human guinea pig. Stupendous results! Two thirds of all men, women, and children in the United States now take prescription drugs.

Linking the primary cause of mental illness to biochemical imbalance, the fabricated scientific evidence of a depression gene—or any other curable culprit—is, indeed, a brilliant marketing strategy. By removing the spotlight away from the socioeconomic scene, pharmaceutical companies and their cohorts have developed a highly profitable quick-fix scheme for a problem that is

[83]

as complex as the mental disorders their drugs attempt to suppress. The grim sociological circumstances that contribute to the development of mental illnesses are kept in the back shadows of the health care debate stage; like haunting voices echoing through the dark caves of a disturbed mind. In the end, the mental illness is failing to realize that the socioeconomic culture has become schizophrenic and in desperate need of psycho-emotional treatment.

In fair democratic fashion, it is not only the average slave-wage workers constantly imperiled by unemployment and immersed in mounting debt who become victims of mental illness. The wealthy, too, are inflicted with a vast array of mental and emotional disorders. The main distinction between the opposing class groups is that the well-to-do has access to the best health care services money can buy, whereas the cash-depleted and debt-ridden average worker with no health insurance falls deeper into mental agony, which can often lead to crime. While the rich can afford medical visits with high-fee psychotherapists who prescribe costly drugs, the poor resorts to traditional home treatment that can involve alcoholic beverages, illegal drugs, and even domestic violence as a form of stress-relief therapy; to the abuser, that is. However, both the rich and poor are susceptible to a complete fallout and pushed to the edge of the abyss of desperation; and once on the brink, they may opt to jump off the cliff and put an end to their miserable existence. Yes, mental illness is more than just a medical condition; it is a social malaise that is democratically distributed among the servants of my system, regardless of their social strata.

The mentally ill population in the United States is as diverse as American society itself. Take, for instance, an idle wealthy investor suffering from the overbearing anxieties brought about by the instability of the stock market. His perturbed mind and emotions may go unnoticed to the public eye, unless, of course, if his indomitable sickened mind turns into a wild horse that gallops away with his common sense trampling basic social norms. Most of the time, however, the expensive therapies and mood monitoring drugs will suppress the mental disturbance and conceal the symptoms of modern madness. On the other hand, the large number of financially stressed citizens, having neither access to health care services nor the pecuniary means to halt the snowballing effects of mental illness, those are buried under the avalanche of poverty and insanity. Unlike their well-to-do fellow-citizens, these population groups end up either in overcrowded private enterprise penitentiaries or the lonely and filthy streets of large urban centers. Once alienated from themselves and society, the very mental illness that wreaked havoc in their lives becomes in itself the palliative that allows them to endure the absurdity of living.

While the mental illness afflicting the affluent often can be traced to its initial manifestations, the origin of the mental disturbance devastating the destitute homeless remains a conundrum. Like the perennial quandary that asks "what came first the chicken or the egg?" it is difficult to determine whether the homeless mentally ill became homeless because he was mentally

ill or if it happened in reverse. Unlike the popular inquiry, however, it is well-known that both alienation
and the overwhelming stress engendered by poverty are
major contributors to mental and emotional dysfunc-
tions. That being the case, a citizen without work, money, education, and the basic necessary means to make a
living, will most certainly end up homeless—or incar-
cerated—and alienated from a society whose values are
determined by economic functions and accumulation of
wealth. Left alone and neglected, these individuals become the human trash dirtying the streets of populous
urban centers where multitudes of people pass by them
with utmost indifference—and even contempt. Lo the
mental illness of the downtrodden hatches out of the
egg of poverty.

In the profitable industry of sickness the raw material of prosperity is, of course, sickness itself. And there
are countless arrays of illnesses from which to extract
handsome revenues. They range from the common cold
and allergy to malign tumors and paralyzing neurologi-
cal disorders. The possibilities for profit are as varied
as the ailments themselves: medications, treatments,
doctors' visits, laboratory tests, medical supplies, hos-
pitalizations, and the list goes on. However, the more
complex, challenging, and widespread the disease is the
more lucrative it becomes. Hence, cancer is the most
precious stone in the valuable jewelry box of sickness.

12

Unremitting economic expansion is absolutely indispensable for my survival. It is a fundamental necessity of my being. In order to sustain continuous growth, the market must be constantly stimulated with new investment opportunities while creating the ideal circumstances for emerging enterprises to thrive. Among the many high profit yielding business ventures that my system has produced, one of the most successful and profitable is the industry of sickness—also known as the health care industry, as referred by those who resent the harsh language of the true nature of the industry and prefer a more soothing euphemism. It is in this industry that the nature of my economic system generates within itself an abundant supply of raw materials (illnesses) and the necessary infrastructure for amassing exorbitant profits, which is the ultimate goal of Capitalism.

In addition to the daily burdensome stress weighing on the shoulders of my underlings, which contributes to a variety of physical and mental illnesses, the output of my industrial economic system is not limited to superfluous goods for consumption. Like the human digestive system, industrial production has its intestinal tract that eliminates high volumes of carcinogenic waste matter that are released in the atmosphere, soil, and water that inseminate the environment with sickness. It is from this contaminated womb that cancer is born, though this most profitable virulent commodity in the health care industry is also nurtured through unhealthful processed and chemically fertilized foods, harmful products, insalubrious services, among many other items of consumption that my system produces for profit.

The economic value of a devastating disease like cancer cannot be underestimated. Because it can affect any part of the body and rapidly spread to other vital organs, cancer is a goldmine that generates hefty profits for the vitiated industry of sickness. Directly impacting the lives of millions of people, and indirectly disturbing millions more who are the loved ones of the victims of the disease, cancer has become the ominous symbol of a deadly disease and the main health care issue in industrial societies. It is a frightening ubiquitous illness that is second only to death as a source of anxiety and fear regarding health. With so much at stake, the economic value of this infirmity is astronomical. After all, what's the fair market value of life when it's threatened by such a formidable disease?

Realizing the magnitude of possibilities that cancer offers as a profit-making endeavor, the industry of sickness mobilized its efforts to develop the means to diagnose and treat this physically, emotionally, and financially crushing disease. Consequently, much progress has been made in oncology and the corporate-owned—often times disguised as nonprofit organizations—factories of health care (hospitals, clinics, pharmaceuticals, etc.) set up the comprehensive infrastructure to cash in this extremely profitable misfortune. However, the reason cancer allows for exceptionally high earnings is because of the high cost to diagnose and treat the disease. That is to say, the millions of people without health care insurance—and even the ones who do but lack sufficient financial resources— will not be able to afford the chance to fight for survival. Well, tough luck! In my economic system, health care is a luxury commodity that is on the market for those who can afford it. As for those who can't, I ought to remind them that they are replaceable cogs in my complex machinery of production; many die and many more are born to replace them. That's what overpopulation is for. That's why I maintain a large army of labor reserve.

If I sound mean-spirited and indifferent to the plight of those who succumb to a dreadful disease like cancer is because I am. It is the nature of The Beast to be indifferent to the problems of others. After all, I'm all about greed, selfishness, and competition for higher profits. My creator, Adam Smith, made it very clear that it is the pursuit of self-interest that leads to the common good. Therefore, the CEOs of the factories of health care and pharmaceutical corporations, as well as the medical doctors, the laboratory technicians, and everyone else involved in the lucrative industry of illness, they are all minding their own self-interest, which demonstrates my demands for unbridled consumption is the pursuit of happiness.

But I'm not as nefarious as I seem. The stalwart adherents of my economic system are responsible enough to recommend that women get mammograms and pap smears on a regular basis. They also advise everyone over the age of 50 to undergo a colonoscopy procedure in order to detect the early signs of colon cancer, which significantly reduces the risk of death by this disease. What they cannot do, however, is to violate the fundamental principles of my system by neglecting their own self-interests or focus their attention on the welfare of others. Hence, if single mothers making minimum wage must choose between feeding their children or getting an annual breast exam, it is not the responsibility of my system to care for their needs. Same is applicable to a poor senior citizen with precarious medical history who cannot afford to pay for the cost of the recommended colonoscopy. My lackeys' loyalty and commitment must always be to me—and to themselves of course—but never to their brothers and sisters in distress. For Gold sake, Capitalism is fueled by the pursuit of profit in a competitive environment, not compassion in a cooperative mode of existence. I am about profits, not utopia.

The obstinate critics of my economic system suffer from prosperity myopia. They cannot see that Capitalism is not only the most financially viable web of commerce to create wealth, but also the quintessence of a democratic approach to business. As it is well advertised, in my propaganda apparatus, there is opportunity for all to pursue their self-interest and achieve their financial dreams. In spite of the evidences to the democratic approach of my economic system, the vitriolic foes of Capitalism argue that only a privileged few ever succeed while the majority scrambles to eke out a mediocre living. Their argument only shows another myopic perception. Of course only a few will succeed! After all, it is a highly competitive system; and the end result of competition is the inevitability of winners and losers. Nevertheless, the economic twist to democratic principles is solidly in place to validate my sovereignty.

Let them say what they wish. I couldn't care less for what my critics think is unjust. It's been repeated ad nauseam that under the fair and free market system everyone has a chance to succeed. Be it access to health care, equal opportunities, delivery of justice, and an array of limitless professional opportunities are equally available and open to everyone in society—and so is The Ritz-Carlton Hotel.

13

There are many lovers who legitimize their commitment to each other through the sacrosanct institution of marriage. I, too, have established a committed marital relationship with my lover and supporting partner. But unlike traditional lovers, my engagement has absolutely nothing to do with love and devotion. Of course not! That would contradict the fundamental principles of my economic system. Instead, my union is based on reciprocal exchange of interests—what social scientists define as social exchange theory, which is the involvement in relationships that provide rewards or profits. Also, in order to spice up the marriage, I invited a long-time lover of mine to join in the relationship. Together, the three of us have formed the dirtiest *ménage a trois* in the political history of the world.

I admit that it was an arranged marriage of interests. From the very beginning of my inception as a dominant socioeconomic force, I've been aware that the nature of Capitalism is antagonistic to human nature, thus I've always felt threatened by rebellions that could lead to overthrowing my way of life. Consequently, like imperial monarchs arranged marriages in order to establish alliances that strengthened their position in the constant struggle for power, I realized that I desperately needed a solid partnership to safeguard and validate my existence. And no one could better serve my cause than that most beautiful lady whom humanity reveres as if she were a sacred goddess. In her turn, she also needs me to consolidate her lofty ideals and morals through material prosperity for societies that embrace her principles. It was a perfect combination of interests. Hence, the holy matrimony between Capitalism and democracy was officiated in the courthouse of right-eousness.

Our union was a match made in economics heav-en. The fundamental tenets of my principles fit into hers like a phallic jigsaw puzzle piece. Free enterprise, *laissez-faire* (allow to do), pursuit of self-interest; vir-tually all the staples of my economic dogma agree with her social organizational principles: Freedom, allowing citizens to participate, pursuit of happiness, and many of her values find a corresponding parallel in my ways of conducting business. And besides complementing each others' features, we also solidified the lawfulness of our positions in the hearts and minds of men, wom-en, and children. Theoretically, our consecrated part-nership is God-given rights to humanity. In practice, it is the most cunning disguise of the devil to destroy life on earth while lacerating the human spirit.

Once our relationship was sailing through the smooth sea of social acceptance and moderate stability, I brought into the scene my long-time lover who was eager to join my partner and me in the wily scheme to hoodwink humanity. The goal was to turn the pseudo intelligence-gifted species into the antithesis of critical thinking and intellectual independence, which trans-formed them into passive participants in a quasi-fraudulent decision-making process. Thus, after enlisting my lover to the cause, the three of us formed an authoritative triumvirate of domination: Capitalism, democracy, and large corporations. The latter acts as the executive branch of the alliance and is represented in the public arena in two distinct forms: lobbyists and politicians.

As I do with everything else under my domain, I turned democracy, my legitimate marital partner, into a commodity as well—many claim that I've prostituted her as if I were a street pimp. But first I had to do some tweaking with the original Greek concept of direct democracy and mold it to meet my needs. The idea of having important political decisions happening at the local level, as it happened in some ancient Greek-city-states, posed a serious danger to my security, for organized individual citizens convening is small decision-making groups for the interest of their local communities would likely conflict with the generalized interests of my economic system. The awareness of this looming menace propelled me to take action as soon as The Industrial Revolution began. Thus, during the 18th and 19th centuries I stimulated the new concept of representative democracy in which the central institution is the representative parliament where decisions are effected by majority vote. However, in order to ensure that the perceived nobility of democracy remained impervious to external influences, I had to establish dignified approaches to representative democracy: regular elections with free choice of candidates, universal adult suffrage, freedom to organize rival political parties, independence of the judiciary, freedom of speech and the press, and the preservation of civil liberties and minority rights, among other characteristics. Although it may seem at first that these liberties could jeopardize the safety of socioeconomic oppression, the marriage of Capitalism to democracy compels the alienated populations to oblige to my system's whims.

As the rightful husband of the beautiful lady representing the will of the people, I transformed her nature to my advantage. In an economic system like mine in which the selfish pursuit of profit is the ultimate goal, everything is fair game; even hallowed institutions and beliefs. Thus, the demoralization of democracy came about effortlessly, albeit tantamount to transforming a loving and devoted housewife into a crass street whore. Yes, I've prostituted democracy and I am not ashamed of it; to the contrary, I'm proud of turning myself into the pimp of the entire political system.

Prostitution, either of the human physical body or a revered institution like democracy, is profitable business. Unlike the illegal practice of hawking sex on the streets, marketing and selling democracy is not only legal but also a necessary commercial practice to garner legitimate support for my existence. And as sophisticated means of mass-communications evolved through technological advancement, monopolizing the channels through which information is disseminated was an imperative requisite for manipulating public opinion. Thus, it was a matter of time for my system to propitiate the circumstances for all major broadcasting networks from print to electronic media to be corporate-controlled by means of private ownership. Even small towns newspapers and radio stations must belong to giant news media corporations in order to exercise influence and control at the local level, regardless of the size of the community.

After taking over the means of mass-communication to control the flow of information, a pervasive propaganda campaign advertising inalienable rights ensues. The ultimate goal is to inculcate the theoretical conviction that freedom, justice, equality of opportunities and rights, among other democratic concepts, are the solid foundation upon which a free market society stands. Once the masses are made believe that they are free they become free by self-conviction, even when their daily experience contradicts their belief system. Like the religions and gods that they created and follow blindly, the seductive allure of lofty moral principles intoxicates their senses, as they surrender their intellectual freedom to the slavery of propaganda or mythological chimera. Little they know that in my economic system even freedom is a commodity; a luxury item that only a few can afford to buy.

Just as freedom has become a coveted commodity, democracy is now a tawdry commercialized institution engendered by political activities. I managed to turn democracy into a sub-market within the free market economic system in which beneficial political decisions are made on my behalf. Indeed, I have prostituted the noble lady and demand her to go out peddling her services for the highest bidder. However, I am well aware of the importance of deluding the Johns into believing that they are the ones making all the major decisions through their elected representatives, even though less than half of the eligible voters participate in the so-called democratic process. It's actually remarkable how they can accept as a veritable fact that they live in a free democratic society; and yet, the majority is not convinced that their votes can have any significant weight in the outcome of elections.

As a ramification of the free market economic system, democracy has its own currency called the vote. It is a unique exchange modality for consumption of political goods. Being an important partner of the economic system, it must emulate the fundamental principles of the system; that is, the pursuit of self-interest. Thus, in the free election market of democracy, politicians are motivated by their own self-interest in serving as representatives of the people who will purchase their services with the vote-currency. However, even though voters cash in political candidates, the ownership of the elected officials' loyalty belongs not to voters, but to those who financed their high-priced political campaigns. Even wealthy citizens aspiring for public office by investing large sums of their own fortunes in the pursuit of their political aspirations, they, too, owe allegiance to business associates linked to the source of their wealth. After all, the political structure plays a critical role in the sustainability of the free market economic system; therefore it must be controlled by powerful business groups.

Politicians are one of the most expensive—though often times utterly worthless—commodities for sale on the sub-market of democracy. And regardless of their personal reasons for running for public office, there is one thing they generally share in common: they are in it for themselves; and denying it is to refute the backbone

principle of the pursuit of self-interest that they adamantly defend. Who could blame them? In most situa-
tions, it's a well-remunerated job with excellent "benefits" and great potential for collateral rewards. No
wonder they are willing to invest much time, energy,
and even their own money in grueling political campaigns that expose them to the limelight of the public
eye. The novices in the business of politics do everything they can to pave the way for a self-serving long
advantageous political career. They may start out their
ambitions by pursuing membership in local businesses,
school boards, and other community organizations'
board of directors in order to gain visibility and solidify
their credentials as public servants. Once they establish
their positioning as viable public figures, they venture
to compete against recognized professional politicians.
However, if the aspiring politician can garner support
from powerful interest groups, even a neophyte with no
related experience can become the trusted representative of the people. In fact, this has become the new
trend in the marketplace of democracy.

When the time of the year comes for the disheart-
ened populace to shop with their vote-currency for a
candidate that might restore hope in their dismal lives,
the career politicians launch comprehensive advertisement campaigns. In well thought-out marketing strategies, they elevate their inconsequential aptitudes while
smearing the reputation of their competitors. But in
order to raise the necessary resources to finance the
costly aspiration to land a profitable seat in public office, they must sell themselves and their political agenda to private interest groups interested in investing in

their political campaigns. At a later date, the financiers return to claim the interests accrued in their investment in the political stocks of the purchased elected official. Lo in the sub-market of democracy politicians are commodities advertised to a despondent electorate each with only one vote-currency to spare—and most don't even spend it.

Displayed in elaborate formats and filled with persuasive slogans, the political marketing materials convey optimistic and patriotic messages intended to persuade the distraught consumer of democracy to purchase the chosen public representative other interest groups already own. Once elected, they become the champions and spokespersons for the causes of the interest groups that financed their expensive political campaigns. Therefore, even in the sub-market of democracy in which the vote is supposed to be the prevailing currency for purchasing commodity political candidates, it is still the good old money that buys illusory democratic elections.

As an integral part of the free enterprise economic system, the free elections democracy market bears numerous similarities to the mother system. In the business of democracy, as in any other traditional commercial activity, it doesn't matter how worthless the political product is as long as it is deceitfully wrapped in the decorative illusion of competence delivered through suggestive marketing strategies. Like the superfluous products of consumption that depend on creative advertisement campaigns in order to boost sales, in the power yielding business of politics candidates must sell their public appeal to apathetic and alienated voters desperate for a quick-fix solution for their interminable social, economic, and political ills. That's how public representative products are bought and sold in the democracy market, which lacks both integrity and majority participation. Thus, in order to succeed in the competitive political environment where well-funded opponents bombard the electorate with advertisements, those coveting to offer their favors in what has become the brothel of democracy must cajole the sponsorship of influential corporate pimps controlling the prostitution of democracy. As for the alienated citizens, they get their fleeting satisfaction out of participating with their ineffectual vote in a corrupted process they cannot influence with the undervalued currency of the democracy market. Under my system, democracy has become a high stake game that only big gamblers have a seat at the table of power.

The development of this political trend has evolved over the years in order to discourage the involvement of legitimate men and women of leadership. My economic system cannot afford to allow authentic leaders who are genuinely concerned with the welfare of the people to take public office, for they'd pose a veritable threat to the pursuit of selfish interest principle that rules free market economy.

Hence, I had no choice but to prostitute the beautiful lady to guarantee my longevity. However, before turning democracy into a vulgar political harlot, I first had to defile the meaning of community that society needs for genuine democracy to thrive.

14

At a time long erased from the collective memory of modern industrialized societies, humanity used to prosper in tribalism. The ideological concept sustaining tribal consciousness was based on unwavering commitment to the welfare of the tribe and every single member of the group. Despite the hierarchical structure that prevails in the social organization of tribes, the leaders of the tribal community were aware of their responsibility to promote the common good. They knew that, like an infected toe nail can disease the entire body, if even one member of the tribe was troubled, the whole community would suffer the consequences. This communal-consciousness calls for a spirit of unhindered cooperation, which is the antithesis of the tenets of my economic system that demands unfettered competition among greedy individuals in the selfish pursuit of profit. Thus, unable to coexist with the primitive morals of a culture of poverty, I had no choice but to besmirch the values of community integration.

As any good military strategist knows, once you conquer the strongest faction of resistance in the enemy's front, the remaining forces will fall like a domino effect. Attentive to this important strategic detail, I initiated the spreading of my ways in the New World of America, which would later become the Mecca of Capitalism, by obliterating the Native American tribes and their cultures. Besides their community-oriented approaches that contradicted head on the competitive nature of my economic development in the new land—their land—of opportunity, their reverence to the life-sustaining environment not only obstructed the exploration of abundant natural resources for profit, but also posed a consciousness threat to my existence with future generations. However, even though I ensured that they were either killed, confined to reservations, or at least partially acculturated to my way of living, those brute savages who worship animals, plants, trees, and poverty managed to keep their tribal and nature-loving consciousness alive in the collective subconscious mind of modern civilized societies. I should have heeded the pledge of that Shawnees Chief, Tecumseh, who cried out:

> "Where today are the Pequot? Where are the Narragansett, the Mohican, the Pokanoket, and many other once powerful tribes of our people? They have vanished before the avarice and the oppression of the white man, as snow before the summer sun…Will we let ourselves be destroyed in our turn without a struggle, give up our homes, our country bequeathed to us by the Great Spirit, the graves of our dead and everything that is dear and sacred to us? I know you will cry with me, "Never! Never!"

Perhaps it is true that one can eliminate an individual or culture but never their spirit, for I've been having problems with the persistence of the foolish ideals of nature-loving people who don't understand that they cannot accumulate wealth without consuming the earth. They love their cars, airplanes, computers, televisions, cell phones, and everything else my system bestows upon them. And yet, a growing number of concerned citizens are crying foul against my ways by demanding concern about the earth like I demand their consuming unessential goods. They worry about the forests that are rapidly disappearing under the axes of greed. They cough out their anxiety with the deteriorating quality of air in large urban centers. They seem troubled about the dirty water they drink and the contaminated soil they grow their foods. They lose sleep over the disappearing species of the earth, wondering when they will be next on the extinction list. They fear that they are doomed and that I am the one to blame, and now they are fighting back. Well, let them waste their dwindling energy. I've never lost a battle against opposing forces of my almighty wealth-generating economic system. I either raze the opposition into nothingness or gulp them up and turn them into contributing supporters of my cause. They have no way out: for as long as humankind remains selfish and greedy, I will always be their master.

Once I cleared the plains from the poisonous human weed that Native Americans represent, I paved the way for the development of Industrial Capitalism in the land of the free. However, having learned my lessons about the dangers of cooperative tribal mentality from the savages, I accelerated the process of continuous growth keeping in mind that the cooperative sense of community had to be either eradicated or at least severely compromised. The development of large urban centers was critical for breaking down the ideological concept of communal living, for city dwellers live quasi-incognito from their closest neighbors, though surrounded by millions of people. Their relationships with the members of the community are superficial in general and mostly take place in the exercising of their economic functions.

It is in the lost sense of community that I am found. Workers unconcerned with their neighbors become greedier, more selfish, and more competitive, which improve both productivity and consumption. The invigorated economy ignites a spurt of growth and the songs of praise for my economic system are sung in the four corners of the world. Then, the egoistic self blends in with the culture and turns into a collective egoistic entity that is represented through my activities.

In spite of my confidence in the successes of my suppressing the sense of community inherent in human nature, I must always keep an attentive eye over my shoulder. Although the irrepressible imposition of my way of life has always prevailed, the ghosts of the millions of Native Americans slaughtered for their land and riches still haunt me scared. It's true that I managed to dissolve their culture with the potent weapons of alcohol, gun powder, dynamite, and, of course, Christianity. Nevertheless, I am aware of the legacy they've left behind with their reverence for the earth and all the living creatures on the planet; and this consciousness threatens the sovereignty of my economic system. The menacing words of *Shingis*, a Chief from the Delaware tribe, still echoes in my ears:

THE BEAST

"The white people think we have no brains in our heads. They are great and powerful, and that makes them make war with us. We are but a little handful to what they are. But remember...when you hunt for a rattlesnake, you usually cannot find it—and perhaps it will bite you before you see it."

But I shouldn't feel intimidated. After all, I have triumphantly hunted down many political rattlesnakes that have tried to poison my economic system with primitive tribal concepts of cooperation and reverence for the environment. I have beheaded and skinned numerous of those treacherous reptiles; and I've developed the antidote to their poisons as well—the poison that kills is also the antidote that saves. I've proven throughout history that I am immune to their venom. I've asserted my power and ability to swallow up the opposition and digest them into becoming part of my system. I am above and beyond the interests of the overworked individual, the non-existent community, or this doomed ailing planet. I am invincible and the only thing that will ever demolish me is my own self-destructive process.

And yet, I've been concerned with the safety of my sovereignty. But when I fret about the emerging consciousness calling for environmental preservation, social justice, cooperation, and all the nonsense humanistic approaches that contradict the principles of my economic system, I try to relax recalling my greatest victory ever against a juggernaut opponent. Yes, if I was able to defeat the most awe-inspiring social movement opposing my ways in the annals of modern history, then I know that I can overpower any and all attempts against my supremacy as the forever dominant economic force in the world.

15

Once the ominous clouds of the atomic bombs explosions over Hiroshima and Nagasaki dissipated, an astonished world population realized that an unprecedented dangerous era in the history of human civilization had just begun. It was from the nuclear mushroom that the flower-power generation blossomed.

No matter how hard I tried to bring in new and exciting distractions into the lives of the post-World War II children, they seemed to be growing up quite differently than the pre-nuclear age generations did. Strange, I thought. Their parents lived through a great economic depression and survived the horrors of a devastating world war; but this new batch of human beings, in spite of the prosperity that my lively activated economic system generated by post-war reconstruction investments, they did not display signs of childhood contentment. From their early days, I already could tell that they felt indifferent to the pursuit of wealth and my way of life. Even the technological advancements of the time did not appear to enthrall them as it does the children of the twenty-first century. I wasn't sure whether they were being born like that or perhaps it was the fallout of radiation in the atmosphere of the earth that was affecting their behavior. Whatever the case may be, I began worrying about my future—a lot!

Fretting about what could happen if an entire generation of consumers rebelled against my economic system, I launched an aggressive indoctrination campaign aiming at curbing and thwarting any initiatives that could compromise my existence. Thus, I turned the 1950's into a decade of domestication, complacence, consumerism, and, of course, fear, which has always been the most effective weapon in my arsenal of persuasion. Suddenly, I was elated to notice how my strategy was working so well: eminent happy suburban families consuming a large variety of goods ranging from washing machines to gaseous black sugary drinks; masses of distracted workers glued to television sets, which remains a delightful sight to my vision; submissive women, children, and students who obeyed the commands of their fathers and teachers; working class people contented to have a wage-slave job while consuming themselves to "debt;" and the national fear that the commies were about to take over and nuke Capitalism out of the face of the earth. The latter was like a tornado that swept away the most reverent document of political freedom.

I can't say that I was pleased to witness the nation that basks in the glory of its democratic principles egregiously violate the First Amendment of its Constitution, which guarantees inalienable rights to freedom of speech, press, assembly, petition, and religion to its citizens. After all, I was aware that the undemocratic draconian measures were aimed at safeguarding the interests of my economic system, for the antagonistic model was spreading rapidly around the world like a wild fire. Still, I have to admit that I was astonished by how those constitutional rights were blatantly trampled under the boots of congressional despotism—and I worried that it could have bad repercussions in the long run and hurt my ways. Besides, I knew that my lackey, Senator Joseph McCarthy, had long been exploiting the issue of communism for his own political advantage. But when he set off a witch hunt against citizens who peacefully and rightfully exercised their constitutional rights, I thought he was misusing the effective weapon of fear and taking it to the level of public aggression. For cash sake, even those who pleaded the Fifth Amendment right to remain silent were punished by omission. Labeled as Un-American or communists, a multitude lost their employment, reputation, and life became a living hell in the land of the free. To make matters worse, the usurpation of power carried out by the democratic institutions that are supposed to uphold the Constitution was condoned by a passive and alienated citizenry.

In the meantime, while my political servants carried on the business of persecuting innocent citizens, I was terrified sensing how the youngsters of the dreary 1950s despised the fearful Red scare tactics enacted by their leaders. I was watching those teenagers growing up in the shadows of a brutal and devastating world war wondering when the next one would occur. I could see in their eyes that they were losing trust and confidence in both the strength and rightfulness of my economic system and the political apparatus that keeps it in place. I was scared for my safety. Then, on the first day of 1959 when a small revolutionary guerrilla band overthrew an allied dictatorship, I realized that would be some rough times ahead. Indeed, the most dangerous and threatening time in the entire history of the sovereignty of Capitalism and its way of life was about to begin. It was a decade that would put to the test the resilience and strength of my economic system. Although I ultimately prevailed—as I always do—it was a major cultural battle that pushed me to the brink of annihilation.

Watching the children of the well-to-do celebrate the victory of a bunch of cigar-smoking bearded rebels was an eyebrow-raising experience. I remember hearing the echoes of "Viva La Revolucíon!" on the campus of prestigious universities where the privileged youth was educated. I am not sure that they knew what they cheering for, though I am positive that it had more to do with opposition to me than support for the fall of a dictatorship overseas. They were initiating a home-based rebellion of their own to show their contempt for unfettered consumerism. They were fed up with the assault on their constitutional rights that the McCarthy era exemplified, as well as the social injustices committed against the poor and underprivileged populations. They were appalled with the unacceptable segregation policies toward minority groups—a violation of another constitutional right, the Fourteenth Amendment. Women began realizing that they, too, were relegated to second class citizen status. A new environmental awareness movement started gaining grounds in mainstream culture. Those young devils were on a mission to set out some serious socioeconomic transformations. I'd never witnessed anything like that before; and certainly not coming from the upper echelon of society. They were going mad—and I was growing increasingly anxious.

Suddenly, a serious military crisis knocked on the door of self-destruction. When my nemesis from the east decided to place atomic weapons on the adversary Caribbean island they captured with their political tentacles, the protector nation of my system reacted accordingly. Then, the world stared down into the dismal abyss of a possible atomic war holocaust with endless nuclear winters to come.

In addition to aggravating the military tension between the two opposing superpower nations, the crisis also contributed to enforcing the peace-oriented agenda of that generation, for now more than ever they realized how close the world was to total obliteration. And as the war against communism in Southeast Asia escalated in numbers, rage, and deaths, the rebelling youth intensified their resistance and struggle against, not only the war, but also my economic interests that motivated the atrocities. Suddenly the war subdivided itself into two distinct fronts: the military battlefields against communism abroad, and the social war against the principles of Capitalism at home.

Like a fire spreading through the prairies, the hot flames of social discontent reached faraway lands igniting an international upheaval against the *status quo*. The movement was so insidious and widespread that penetrated even the symbolic iron curtain of the blocknations that opposed my economic system. It was a transcontinental mess: pandemonium at university campuses, brutality and murder of protesters, vile and violent military dictatorship regimes taking over demo-

[111]

cratically elected governments under the auspices of the leader-nation of the free world, assassinations of civil rights leaders and popular political figures, massacres, persecutions and prosecutions everywhere. It was global chaos. And there I was, standing at the epicenter of this sociological earthquake wondering whether I'd fall in the crevice of unruliness and be consumed into oblivion.

By 1964 the gates of the American Counterculture Revolution had burst right open at the Sather Gate on the Berkeley campus of the University of California where students were prohibited to distribute pamphlets. Since they had demonstrated in the past against the egregious constitutional rights violations carried out by the House of Un-American Activities Committee at San Francisco City Hall, the enforced prohibition was the *coup de grace* to their tolerance. Thus, soon afterwards, the students took over Sproul Hall on campus as a symbolic enactment of people's rights to access public property. It was the starting point of the Free Speech movement that spread across America and had repercussions around world. But when the students decided to designate a specific area to build a "People's Park," the opposition forces crushed their ambition. By that time the light at the end of the counterculture revolution tunnel started dimming piecemeal.

In the meantime, the escalation of the war in the jungles of Southeast Asia intensified the youth rebellion while heightening the domestic crisis. Assassinations of prominent political and civil rights leaders, murder of protesting students on university campuses, organization of minority urban militia demanding power and social justice, among dozens of other infamous events featuring on primetime news media broadcast sent a wave of insecurity and fear across a traumatized nation. Chaos ruled the streets of a culturally battered society.

For the first time, I experienced what it was like to be on the receiving end of the impact of a fear-driven environment; something that until then I'd only known as a self-benefiting weapon that I wielded to manipulate the masses in order to perpetuate my existence. Suddenly, I felt the sharp deadly blade pressed against my own throat, as a blood-thirsty rebellious youth seem ready to slash the carotid artery of Capitalism.

Like the Luddites of the early Industrial Revolution who revolted against the machinery that robbed them from their work and livelihood, the post World War II generation acted as their counterparts but in the social, economic, political, and cultural arenas. They were determined to tear asunder the constitutional principles of Capitalism, destroy my way of life, and replace it with a new social order based on cooperation, freedom, equality, and communal living; the antithesis of everything I stand for. The rebelling rascals favored simplicity over opulence and began promoting the new lifestyle by exemplification. They tried to ruin consumerism by establishing a new fashion trend in which worn out blue jeans and simple old clothing were the desired looks of the epoch. They established independent self-sustaining communes with the purpose of breaking away from traditional consumerism life style. They called one another "brothers and sisters," just like the commies addressed themselves as comrades. They became a force to be reckoned with and therefore had to be swiftly eliminated.

The aftershocks of this sociological earthquake taking place in the heartland of Capitalism was being felt everywhere on earth. Even some of my long-standing allies were negatively influenced to the point of turning against me. Christianity in general and the Catholic Church in particular, institutions that I'd long relied on to uphold the principles of my economic system, were beginning to show signs of disunity and weakness. Rebellious theologians in Latin America, a continent ravaged by poverty and social injustices, came up with the preposterous idea that they were supposed to follow the living example of Jesus of Nazareth. Thus, because Jesus lived a simple life serving the poor, the sick, the exploited, and the oppressed—the members of his community, that is—those idealistic priests surmised that they should emulate the example of their spiritual leader. They baptized the new religious movement Liberation Theology. It posed a serious threat; not only to my existence, but to the domination of the Christian Church in the region as well.

Soon it was as though there was a civil war within the Christian Church. On one side stood the traditional Christian values epitomized by the imposing figure of the Pope in his regalia and gold ornate environment. On the other side, contrasting with the opulence and dogmatic political stance of the Church, the humbly clad priests roaming the countryside of poverty-stricken regions offering services and hope for the destitute—like their spiritual leader did. The contrast in behavior between the traditional Church and its rebellious priests was evident and troublesome. And to make matters worse, Liberation Theology was increasingly welcomed by both a new generation of clergies, as well as disadvantaged populations who perceived the movement as a genuine Christian-like endeavor. They began realizing the hypocrisy of Latin American dominated Catholic Church, which the Pope is but a king of the Vatican Empire. This awakening of consciousness opened their eyes for the equally hypocritical elements of the socioeconomic and political system that ruled their lives. For me, it was time to fight back with a vengeance.

Sacrilegious to Capitalism, Liberation Theology had to be purged by a newly established form of inquisition. Like in medieval Europe, where the faithful who disagreed with the erroneous inviolable truths of the Church were persecuted and burned at the stake, in the second half of the twentieth century in Latin America those who disagreed with the hallowed concept of free market were persecuted, prosecuted, and often times tortured to death. Young Christian priests committed to emulating the living example of Jesus, the source of their religious inspiration, were branded as communists; the most dangerous political blasphemy of the era in the region. Hunted down—sometimes literally— they went underground and became a vilified religious group now demoted to political status. A high ranked figure in this movement was quoted as saying: "When I feed the poor, they call me a saint. When I question why the poor doesn't have food, they call me a communist."

In the meantime, the two very different major war fronts of the time raged on unabated: the struggles against communism and consumerism. While the former was fought in military style with deadly firearms and weapons of oppression, the latter was carried out through peaceful protests and significant lifestyle change. As the counterculture movement progressed, it produced a new social class composed of a peculiar category of citizens: the hippies. The anti-consumerism militants were mostly middle-class and educated youngsters who strove to revolutionize a new culture by changing traditional social norms. They created all sorts of problems to my economic system. The young bastards whom I'd conscripted into my reserve army of labor, all of a sudden they not only abandoned their economic function duties to my system, but also turned into deserters of my active army of consumers. Although my lackeys always emphasized the concept of freedom as an important element of economic and political propaganda, the culture-change revolutionaries tagged the word freedom as one of the main staples of their social and political agenda. But in their quest for freedom what they created was a social bacchanalia.

In a drug-induced frenzy, the young rebels called out for freedom through a myriad of revolutionary causes. From social revolution to sexual liberation, the mind-altered youth demanded the establishment of a new and more comprehensive paradigm for freedom. They were uninterested in free enterprise in a free market society orchestrated by an invisible hand attached to corporate bodies. They'd grown disillusioned with the theoretical freedoms of the First Amendment of their constitution, for they had learned the lessons that Senator Joseph McCarthy taught the nation, as well as their own experience with the repressive response to the expression of their freedoms. They longed for real freedom; the one that has no barriers or limitations; the one that is unattainable. Incapable of obtaining individual and social liberties, they created a utopian world of their own. They indulged in psychedelic experiences, orgiastic sex, and radical artistic expressions, among other manifestations of their pent-up dissatisfaction with the *status quo*. In essence, they followed the motto of the time: "Turn on, tune in, and drop out."

And drop out they did. Like the smoke spewing from the factories, the counterculture revolution faded away and mingled with the existing polluted behavior of society. As for the flower-power generation, the rebel students, the minority militias, the hippies, and all the elements of a turbulent era, they all became but folkloric characters and tales of a bizarre historical time. From their distorted shadows, I emerged stronger and more influential than ever before.

What a waste of precious productive time that was. All the wars they fought against me proved to be futile in the face of my resilience to any violation of my economic system and its consecrated values. As I do with everything within the reach of my tentacles, I turned nearly all of the counterculture initiatives into commodities for profit and allies to my cause, including the participants themselves. Old worn out jeans became vogue, and to this day they are produced in used up appearance with a high price tag. I am grateful to the sexual revolution that liberated men and women to ex-

plore their sexuality openly, for it facilitated the crea-
tion of the multi-billion dollar pornographic industry.
Even the mind-altering drugs indirectly contributed to
dizzying profits in the pharmaceutical industry, for it
inspired the production and advertisement of mood-
altering drugs that generate astronomical profits for
wealthy stockholders. And as the defeated warriors of
the love and peace generation succumbed to my overwhelming power, I coerced them to submit and surrender to my way of life without resistance. The only thing
left for them to do was to serve me with unwavering
commitment and dedication. They had no choice but to
oblige to my demands, unconditionally.

Toward the end of the 1960s, when it was becoming obvious that the economic forces of Capitalism
were insuperably stronger than the ideals of a cooperative and humanitarian society, the young heroes of ide-
alism gradually saw their movement come to the brink
of demise. In the face of disappointment and a certain
degree of desperation, the retreating army of counterculture revolutionaries split into two factions: one
group turned to spirituality and mysticism in an attempt
to maintain the social values they embraced. The other
contingent deserted the cause and sold themselves
cheap in the free market in the pursuit of profit. The
latter group granted me ineffable personal satisfaction.
Witnessing the adamantly rebellious hippies of the
1960s turn into the superficial dandy yuppies of the
1980s was one of my greatest victories.

Although I was able to overcome the most treacherous decade in the history of Capitalism, the voices
crying out for social, economic, and political transfor-

[118]

mation still echoes in the polluted atmosphere. They just don't seem to go away. In spite of my ability to eradicate the weeds of the counterculture revolution, the seeds remained deeply embedded in the social soil waiting for the right season to sprout. And as the urgency with ecological preservation surpasses the enthusiasm with economic prosperity, the damn seeds planted in the 1960s have started germinating again. The environmental movement has been vociferously loud in the twenty-first century, which makes me uneasy about my future.

Thus, as I exercise my dominance in the world, I have to suppress and conquer one final uprising against my ways. This insurgence, too, shall be crushed and absorbed into my economic system to generate handsome profits for investors. It's already working itself out beautifully. I do make one last pledge: when I am done with the environmental movement and convert it into an additional trendy sub-market of consumption, there will never be another social unrest against me again.

There will be nothing at all.

16

When I pulled out the toxic weeds of the counter-culture movement from the social soil, I turned it into compost to nourish my own private garden. However, when I was sure that I had extirpated the threat against my economic system, it proved to be the biggest mistake of my greatest victory. As even a neo-phyte gardener knows, it's not enough to yank wild plants out of the ground; one has to poison it to death to make sure that it never surfaces again. I've learned my lesson. Thus, I'll treat the ensuing rebellious movement with the same determination of a gardener holding a canister of herbicide—but not before profiting from its demise.

Like the mythical phoenix bird that emerges back to life from its ashes, a new revitalized counterculture movement emerged under the guise of a New Age. Boding the transformation of society while eliminating the existence of my socioeconomic system in the pro-cess, the New Age movement was not as nearly as treacherous as its predecessor of the 1960s. Unlike the deep-seated social and political agenda of the flower power generation, this offshoot movement of the psy-chedelic revolution was of a different nature; a quasi-religious Western movement influenced by Eastern traditions. Although the origin of the New Age movement can be found in the 18th and 19th centuries, particularly through some esoteric doctrines, my interest in it is limited to my concern with my perpetuation in the dominant culture; and for this purpose, only post-1960 era is relevant to me. Since the movement's motivational drive for social transformation comes from spiritual awakening instead of socioeconomic and political reforms, I did not have the slightest concern with its ability to overthrow my ways. In fact, I saw in it an extraordinary commercial opportunity to generate handsome profits for my entrepreneurial servants.

William Blake, the mystic Englishman poet and painter, used the term New Age in 1809 to describe a coming era of spiritual and artistic advancement. The term has endured through two centuries and became the moniker of a subculture whose ideas and values sprouted out of the counterculture of the 1960s. By the mid-1970s a wave of this subculture had already crashed on the shores of mainstream society and it began moving inland toward a more spiritual social consciousness. The new alternative subculture was proliferating a vast array of esoteric practices: meditation, channeling, psychic and astrology readings, crystal healing, vegetarian diets, holistic health, among other unorthodox social customs. The increasing popularity of this politically harmless movement made me realize the tremendous economic potential at hand: a new emerging market with a committed consumer-based clientele. Unlike the anti-consumerism activists of the 1960s, this New Age group offered no menace to my sovereignty; much to the contrary, they were to become important cogs in my machinery of production and consumption. Instead of suppressing the movement, I absorbed it into my ways effortlessly and with gusto.

The New Age movement, like everything that succumbs to the inescapable magnetic pull of the black hole of Capitalism, surrendered to the tantalizing seduction of profit-making opportunities. Soon the new playing field was inundated with countless philosophers of hypocrisy, would-be healers, bogus psychic seers, pseudo-enlightened gurus, and all sorts of charlatans trying to create a niche in the latest lucrative market. The flood gates were wide opened: publications, businesses, corporations, healing facilities, and a whole new economic world came into being. But this was not the dawning of the Age of Aquarius that mystical visionaries claimed would raise the level of consciousness on the planet. To the contrary, it was the confirmation that the perennial Age of Capitalism was indestructible. In the modern version of the new A.C. era, the only thing rising that matters is profit; the only worthwhile consciousness is the awareness of the importance of the individual's interests above those of the group to which he belongs. There was nothing new about the movement. In fact, it was so common place that I started calling it "The New Page movement;" as just another page in my history book.

Not only I've been utterly unconcerned about any danger this movement may pose to the stability of my economic system, I have the utmost contempt for it. Unlike the peace and love youth of decades yonder, though I hate them for attempting to destroy me, I must say that I have a modicum of respect for the genuine manner in which they carried out their agenda and activities for social transformation. They lived, exemplified, and sacrificed themselves for the changes they wanted to see. It was not at all the same with the quasi-religious approach of the New Age movement. More concerned with the individual's self-interest in spiritual pursuits than the development and welfare of society—in this context the movement epitomizes the egoistic principles of my system—the new cultural fad did not resemble its counterculture revolution roots. Once again, I managed to transform a potentially perilous movement into a money-making machine in which esoteric practices, mysticism, and saccharine philosophies became both cogs in the production process, as well as trivial items of consumption. In the end, all rebellious social forces end up as additional functional components of my economic system.

Following on the footsteps of the New Age movement came the ecological movement. Not nearly as intimidating as the counterculture revolution—but definitely more menacing to my interests than its immediate predecessor—the environmentalists concern me because they carry out their agenda based on the observable ecological distress of the planet. However, my loyal and devoted followers adamantly refute the scientific evidences corroborating the harm that Industrial Capitalism imposes on the environment, for they know that acknowledging guilt compromises society's support for my economic system. In spite of the brouhaha, I am not in the least concerned with this latest social rebellion against my ways. Besides, the gullibility of the "go green group" is nothing short of pathetic.

I classify them into two particular groups: the violence-driven and the active-ineffective.

As it is common in any social movement, there'll always be a few radical individuals and groups who act out their political agenda through violent means. Thus, the ecological movement also has its hardcore factions labeled as terrorist organizations. Carrying out notorious acts of sabotage or sheer destructive attacks known as ecoterror, these activists who think of themselves as rescuers of the embattled planet earth, apparently don't realize that they weaken their cause by giving a bad reputation to the movement they claim to represent. In one particular case that greatly benefited my cause, a well-educated former professor of a prestigious university turned into a revolutionary against technology and its nefarious consequences to the welfare of humanity and the environment. Engaging in terrorist acts that involved murder, this deranged man of knowledge became the poster boy of the extremist tactics against untrammeled economic expansion supported by a technological infrastructure. Rather than stopping the powerful economic wheel from spinning forward, this sociopath and his kin helped solidifying my position in society. They are my allies in reverse.

In my turn, I rejoice every time environmental grassroots organizations block roads to logging sites, destroy technological and research centers, commit arson at motor vehicles dealerships, or any other wanton attacks in what they perceive to be symbolic representations of my economic system's contribution to ecological damage. The reason I celebrate those acts of terrorism is because they strengthen my position in the eyes of a disapproving society. They marginalize the entire environmental movement by tainting its reputation as disorderly. Furthermore, it offers my lackeys the opportunity to criminalize the activists and denigrate the reputation of the ecological movement as a collective social pariah. Consequently, I not only conquer the violence-driven brand of environmental activism, but I also use them to consolidate my position as a catalyst for social order against senseless hostility.

The other category of the ecological movement activism, the active-ineffective group, is equally harmless but more of a nuisance than its violence-driven counterpart because they don't make themselves a stigma to society. As far as my long-term interests are concerned, they are utterly undisruptive in behavior, speech, and action. They are like a tiny pebble in the shoe of Capitalism; a nagging presence that distracts the mind but not bad enough to stop the running of my economic system. They bother but do not disrupt. They talk loud but into deaf ears. They see but with the blind mind's eye. They move but go nowhere. Actually, they amuse me a great deal with their gullibility. I am not in the least concerned with their ability to put even a small dent on the sturdy armor that protects my economic system. They are but paeans that are eventually sacrificed in the chessboard game I play against the mentally challenged human species.

The active-ineffective group displays peculiar characteristics that are of sociological and psychological nature. Sociologically, they want to believe that the ongoing slaughter of the earth can be halted through their limited local efforts. Among many other preventive actions, they recycle more, drive less, join organizations that support environmental protection, and purchase products from companies capitalizing on the marketing power of green-consciousness. In essence, they do everything within their limited ability to stop the ecological disaster looming on the horizon of industrial civilization. Lo they are so naïve! They actually believe that they can save the earth while keeping me healthy and alive. They don't seem to understand that as long as I exist and thrive, their environment will go in the opposite direction of mine.

Along with the sociological element, the psychological motivation of the environmental preservation movement functions as the fuel that drives forth the activists' actions. Like an antidepressant drug, their small and isolated initiatives make them feel good about themselves, while assuaging the guilt of being a helpless culprit as a cog of my economic system. They are aware of their unwilling and yet inescapable contribution to ecological deterioration by participating in the merry-go-round of consumption. They delude themselves into believing that they're making great progress in rescuing countless doomed species including their own. Aware of both their guilt and social irresponsibility, they make significant changes in their lifestyles. They ride bicycles to the supermarket carrying their own groceries bags to purchase environmentally friendly products whose wrappings and containers they recycle to avoid waste. On the few progressive radio stations, broadcasters encourage their listeners to do what they can to save the earth; and they convey it in a way that sounds like the simplest of missions. What a nincompoopery! How can a supposedly intelligent species also be so gullible?

Truthfully, it does not take deep Hegelian dialectic thinking to figure this out. Let's see: the population is growing at alarming rates along with the economic system that needs to produce increasingly more to meet market demands and create jobs for a multiplying workforce. As both population and the economy expand, so does consumption of natural resources and the sprawling of urban centers. Conversely, the availability of vital commodities such as water for human use and petroleum to run the engine of production, both are depleting rapidly and reaching critical levels of supply. And the more population and the economic system grow, the faster all natural resources will be irreplaceably consumed. Even if the entire world's population implemented an international recycling campaign, which is a utopian possibility considering the widespread ignorance and poverty in third world countries, it still wouldn't keep up with the demands of continuous growth. Besides, there is only so much that can be recycled in a forever expanding socioeconomic system with an insatiable appetite for more—of everything.

Indeed, as long as population and the economic system continue to expand unceasingly, recycling and all the futile efforts to curb the voracious craving for consumption will be for naught. It will serve but the individual's psychological need to quell the guilt of being an accomplice in the destruction of the environment. Hence, the recycling and everything else they do with the intention of salvaging the moribund planet they live in, work only as a self-medicated palliative to

[127]

a guilt-ridden consciousness inspired by a sense of social responsibility. However, deep inside they know that for as long as my economic system of mass-production for consumption and profit rules an over-populated world, neither the earth nor humanity has a long-term chance of survival.

While they carry on their trendy "save the earth" agenda, I delight myself in transmuting their exasperated foolishness into profit-making opportunities for my lackeys. I find it amusing that some people know about the invisible hand that controls the market, but only a few are aware of the existence of my other hand; the one with the magical Midas touch that turns everything into a profit-seeking commercial venture. It is with my King Midas-like hand that I blessed the environmental movement and converted the "greenies" into a whole new army of loyal consumers of a new category of goods: environmentally safe products—and every mainstream business has jumped on this lucrative bandwagon.

After alchemizing the ecological concerns of society using Adam Smith's philosopher's stone, I inaugurated a multi-billion dollar industry catering to this new breed of consumers. It has been fantastically profitable! Green companies, green-friendly products, green-friendly dwellings, green methods of doing business; it is green everything. It is the dominance of the color of money. The business world is becoming greener as fast as the rain forests are becoming grey. What started out as a sub-market niche has now become mainstream business practices with an enormous potential for profit. In fact, companies that do not advertise and promote

themselves as environmental friendly risk lagging behind their green-minded competitors. Even the more
traditional businesses such as supermarket chains must
now have at least one section selling natural products,
lest they lose consumers to the alternative green-
friendly markets emerging everywhere. And even
though the organic and natural products tend to be
much more expensive than the comparable consumer
good, they still manage to attract loyal middle-class
consumers.

Yes, I am the most powerful alchemist that ever
lived, for not only I transform threatening social
movements into golden business opportunities, but I
also turn those who oppose my ways into supporters of
my system; and that's the pinnacle of alchemical prowess. It is the power of Capitalism in action.

Once the marketplace realized the extraordinary
opportunities for capitalizing on the environmental
movement, every single sector of the economic system
boarded on the green-friendly cargo ship to sail to the
new world of the profitable land of green. Large corporations began buying out smaller successful green-
friendly businesses to eliminate the competition and
pave the way for the conglomerate to dominate the
market. Mammoth financial institutions followed suit
offering green-friendly financial products, investments
in ecologically conscious companies, options to invest
mindfully, among other advertisement gimmicks
geared to explore the new market trend. Hardcopies of
paper credit card statements were advertised as detrimental to the environment and the e-statement option
offered to the green-minded consumer who embraced it

wholeheartedly. As a result, millions of dollars in mailing cost savings allowed the same companies to increase the mail delivery of financial products using the same paper they claimed to protect. However, in order to divert attention from the contradiction, the financial corporations make sure that "printed in recycled paper" and "soy ink" are imprinted on the marketing materials mailed out. This simple strategy dispels the contradiction while enticing the environmentally conscious consumer to do business with the company. It's ingeniously deceitful.

As I've proved in my own words, it is impossible to escape the overwhelming power of Capitalism. Every reactionary idea, every social movement, every cultural rebellion, and everything attempted against my system has been taken over, dissected, and transformed into a contributing element. I have evinced the strength and resilience of my economic system since its inception. There is nothing anyone can do to slow, hinder, or stop the forward motion of the juggernaut that I've become. Everything in the world is connected to and depends on me somehow. If I stop growing civilization will come to a screeching halt. If humanity abandons me or let me fail, they will be dragged down into an unprecedented state of social chaos. They are doomed either way.

Alas, the earth and humanity are trapped in the complex web of Capitalism where a wicked black widow spider slowly moves toward its helpless preys. It is just a matter of time before they are devoured.

About the Author

Sebastian de Assis is a writer, teacher, philosopher, and independent scholar with a profound interest in the daunting sociological challenges of his time.

A graduate of the University of Hawaii at Manoa and California State University at Dominguez Hills, he has lived in several countries and traveled extensively through Europe, South and North America, Africa, and the United States. He is fluent in French, Spanish, and Portuguese.

He lives in Oregon where he writes in his personal library while listening to Johann Sebastian Bach, Miles Davis, and other inspiring music that nurtures his spirit.

For more information about Sebastian and his work visit www.sebastiandeassis.com.